The freezing black water closed over Sydney Bristow's head, extinguishing her last hope. She couldn't see, couldn't think. Above her was a small army of gun-toting K-Directorate; below her, darkness and certain death. She was paralyzed by fear.

Suddenly, a hand reached up and grabbed her, pulling her down, down, down, ignoring her feeble attempts to kick. Her final gasp of air burned in her lungs. In less than a minute, she'd have to breathe. Reflex would force her mouth open, and she'd suck down water instead of air. To die like this, in a foreign country, unknown and unclaimed . . .

IN THE DARK . . .

LAURA PEYTON ROBERTS

AN ORIGINAL PREQUEL NOVEL BASED ON THE HIT TV SERIES CREATED BY J. J. ABRAMS

BANTAM BOOKS
NEW YORK * TORONTO * LONDON * SYDNEY * AUCKLAND

Alias: A Secret Life

A Bantam Book / January 2003

ISBN: 0-553-49399-X

Visit us on the Web! www.randomhouse.com

Published simultaneously in the United States and Canada

Bantam Books is an imprint of Random House Children's Books, a division of Random House, Inc. BANTAM BOOKS and the rooster colophon are registered trademarks of Random House, Inc.

PRINTED IN THE UNITED STATES OF AMERICA

OPM 10 9 8 7 6 5 4 3 2

"WHY DO WE HAVE to live in the dorms?" Sydney Bristow complained, lifting her eyes from her Dostoyevsky novel to cast an annoyed glance toward her half-open window. Shouts and laughter tumbled in from outside, riding the warm California breeze. "Freshmen make so much noise."

"In case you've forgotten, *we're* freshmen," Francie Calfo said, twisting around in her chair to gesture with a wet red nail polish brush. She had long since abandoned her studies and was using her desk as a manicure station. "Not only that, but it's Saturday and it's beautiful outside. Any sane person would be out there making noise." Francie's dark brown eyes turned wistful. "Remind me again: Why aren't we out there?"

"Because of me," Sydney said with a sigh. Tossing her book aside on her thin, dorm-issue mattress, she got up to look out the window.

On the freshly mown grass below, students of all ages and descriptions were enjoying the sunny spring day, sitting and talking in groups or playing impromptu games of touch football and catch. Frisbees crisscrossed the scene, and a giggling gang of sorority girls ran back and forth trying to fly a long, colorful kite. Shorts and tank tops were the uniform of the day, and even from her fifth-floor window, Sydney could smell the suntan lotion.

"You should go do something," she said, turning abruptly to Francie. "There's no reason for you to be a prisoner here just because I have to study. With all the hours I've been working, I have to catch up on my classes, but you . . ."

"What kind of friend would I be if I were out having fun while you were here plowing through . . . what are you reading, anyway?" Francie got up and reached for the book Sydney had dropped, lifting its cover by two wet-tipped fingers. "Is this . . . What *is* this?"

Sydney froze. Why had she left that book in plain sight?

"Dostoyevsky," she said quickly. "For my Survey of World Literature class. Everyone has to read it."

She hurried to take the book back, but Francie yanked it out of her reach, arching a disbelieving brow. "In Russian? This *is* Russian?"

"Well . . . yeah, but—"

"I don't want to shock you, Syd, but most lit teachers are fine with students who read the English translation. When did you learn Russian, anyway?"

"I . . . I didn't," Sydney lied. "I mean, I thought I could teach myself. But right now it's giving me the biggest headache. . . ."

At least that part was true.

Francie dropped the book onto Sydney's bed. "I hope you know you're crazy. Between your classes and working at the bank, you don't have enough to do already?"

Sydney smiled weakly, at a loss for an answer.

The worst part is the lying, she thought. *They don't tell you that when you join the CIA. You think the worst part will be the fear, or getting caught, or maybe even dying. But the lying . . . the lying is every day.*

"You're my best friend here, Francie," she blurted out. "You always will be, right?"

Francie laughed, caught off guard. "I haven't put

up with you since last summer just to have you replace me now."

"Never. There's nothing I wouldn't do for you," Sydney said sincerely.

"Except for go outside on a perfectly gorgeous day." Francie pointed hopefully toward the window. "Forget about studying, Syd! Why do we live in L.A. if we never go to the beach?"

"I thought you didn't like your bathing suit."

"That was before I bought a *new* bathing suit. And there's a party tonight at Delt house. I heard some girls talking in the hall."

"A frat party?" Sydney had been to one of those parties early in the year. She had drunk too much and had promptly gotten sick. Since then she'd concluded two things: She definitely wasn't a party girl, and frat boys could be downright disgusting. "Way to talk me into the beach!"

"Really? You'll go?" Francie began waving her hands around, suddenly frantic to dry her red polish. "We can stop by the commons and pick up some sandwiches. And I'll bet I can borrow some beach chairs. I'm pretty sure—"

The pager on Sydney's waistband went off.

"Oh, that is *not* the bank!" Francie exclaimed as Sydney tilted the pager to read the message on its small screen: *Wilson.*

"I'm sorry, Francie. I have to go in."

"But it's Saturday!" Francie protested. "Banks aren't even open on Saturday!"

Sydney gave her an apologetic shrug. "Mine is."

"You have to quit that job! You've only been there a few months and they're already running your life."

"It's probably just some filing," said Sydney, lying again. "Go to the beach without me. If I can get off early, I'll meet you there."

Francie flopped down hard on her bed, disappointed. "You always say you'll get off, but you never do."

"I'll really try this time. But if not, then tonight. All right? I'll definitely be back in time for the party."

"The Delt party?" Francie brightened. "You promise?"

"Only if it makes you very, very happy. You know those frat guys will be drunk and drooling all over us."

Francie smiled, a mischievous glint in her eyes. "I know."

* * *

The downtown street was deserted when Sydney drove her white Mustang into the secure parking garage beneath the Credit Dauphine building. She checked her reflection in the driver's window as she locked the car door: minimal makeup, straight brown hair slicked into a long ponytail, a slightly caught-in-the-headlights look about her brown eyes that she was learning to recognize as excitement. She didn't like lying about her new job, but there was no denying that being an agent-in-training with the CIA was the most exciting thing she'd ever done—not to mention the most important.

As Sydney stepped into the special elevator that would take her to bank sublevel six, hidden headquarters of her true employer, she felt her pulse surge the way it always did when she came to work. If she made it through training, she'd be a spy for a covert branch of the CIA known as SD-6, a full-fledged secret agent dedicated to protecting the United States against all enemies, foreign and domestic. It was an awesome responsibility—and one she was glad to take on. She'd been waiting all her life for a chance to make a difference.

The elevator doors opened and Sydney stepped into a different world. The entrance to SD-6 was a small white room with a single black circle painted on its floor. Sydney strode to the center of the circle, straightened to her full height, and stared directly ahead. Retinal scanning verified her clearance, and a second set of doors opened automatically, admitting her to the main work area.

Raw concrete walls and high dark ceilings gave headquarters a cavelike quality, an impression reinforced by the absence of windows. Fluorescent lights were suspended overhead, but the more interesting illumination came from row upon row of glowing computer monitors on identical nondescript desks.

One of these desks will be mine someday, Sydney thought proudly as she walked past them.

But for now, a scattering of agents she didn't know sat working on projects she wasn't cleared for, keeping the country safe.

"Sydney!" Wilson called, striding out of his office to greet her. Her recruiter and handler at the agency, Wilson was one of the few employees with walls around his desk, even if they were only made of glass. "Op-tech, please. Right away."

Sydney's stomach fluttered as she followed Wilson to the large conference room called Op-tech. Walled off from the surrounding work space, Op-tech had a long table at its center and a flat-screen monitor at every chair to brief agents on their missions.

Why are we sitting in here? Sydney wondered. *Could this be my first real mission?*

But as she took her seat, she noticed that the

monitors were dark. *If I were going on a mission, something would be displayed.*

She was disappointed, but not surprised. She had made huge strides in her training, impressing everyone with her rapid progress, but she was still a long way from knowing everything—and from being a full agent. Training with SD-6 was like taking a second load of college courses, one heavy on languages, geography, politics, and self-defense. She never knew what Wilson would throw at her from day to day, but so far the only thing she hadn't shone at was the immersion tank.

Sydney shuddered, remembering the day a week before when she'd been locked into the small, coffin-like tank that had subsequently been filled with water. She hadn't expected the chamber to fill so quickly or so completely, and when the light had been switched out as well, she had seriously panicked. She had been instructed to hold her breath for three minutes before operating a complicated series of levers to drain the tank and free herself. The embarrassing reality was that she hadn't lasted thirty seconds before she'd started fumbling with the levers—and when the water hadn't drained instantly, she'd hit the emergency release button. Her biofeedback readout had looked like a Richter 8.0 earthquake.

Wilson had been philosophical. "So, you're human after all," he'd said, reading the testing agent's report.

"I . . . don't much like being underwater," Sydney had admitted.

"Why not?"

"I don't know."

But she did know. Her mother had died underwater, in an accident that had sent her car off a bridge when Sydney was only six. Ever since then . . .

"I can swim," she'd reassured Wilson quickly. "I'm a good swimmer. I just . . . usually stay close to the surface."

"Well, you'll have to pass immersion testing eventually," he'd told her, tossing the report onto a pile. "Practice in a pool."

"I will," she'd promised. And she had. But the mere thought of returning to that dark tank . . .

"Have you guessed why I called you in here?" Wilson asked now, easing his stocky form into the chair at the head of the table.

"No."

"I have a mission for you. And I need you to start right away."

Sydney's heart slammed into her rib cage, beating double-time.

"I . . . Good," she said, working to get her

breathing under control. SD-6 taught its agents how to conceal emotion—a life-or-death skill for a spy—but Sydney was still a novice in that department. "That's good."

"You did a great job on that Sandoval thing, and this should be more of the same," Wilson said. "A simple reconnaissance, but one that requires an agent with a certain look. I think you'll be right for it."

Sydney nodded enthusiastically, thrilled by his trust in her. Weeks before, she had successfully taken clandestine photographs of Raul Sandoval, a Cuban rock star suspected of collaborating with the rogue Russian spy group known as K-Directorate. And even though the assignment had turned ugly unexpectedly, Sydney had pulled through with flying colors.

I can do this, she told herself, still trying to regulate her heartbeat. *Whatever it is, I can do it.*

Wilson leaned toward her, the overhead lights picking up the silver in his chestnut hair. "The recon is in Paris."

"Paris!" Sydney exclaimed, forgetting her attempts at calmness. "I've wanted to go there my whole life!"

He checked his watch. "Good. You leave in ten minutes."

"Excuse me?"

The timing couldn't be worse. She had promised Francie she'd meet her at the beach, or at the very least go to that party. But still . . . Paris!

"I mean, okay," she said, amending her outburst. "I just have to run home to pack a suitcase and—"

"No. You leave from *here* in ten minutes."

"But . . . but . . ."

Sydney's thoughts whirled chaotically. She had been hoping to at least leave Francie a note. Then there was the not-so-little problem of what she was wearing. To prove that she really intended to hit the beach later, Sydney had donned a red maillot under her usual bank outfit of a blue button-down shirt and khaki pants. Even now the pressure of the moment was heating her hastily applied sunscreen to full fragrance.

"When will I be back?" she finally asked.

"That depends on how things go. Not for a few days, anyway."

"Oh," she said, her stress level climbing another notch.

Wilson gave her a piercing look. "Is there a problem?"

"No. It's just . . . my roommate will get suspicious if I disappear without telling her anything. And I've got classes."

Taking a cell phone from inside his jacket, Wilson pushed it across the table to her. "That com unit's been assigned to you, for making cover calls to your roommate and anyone else you need to keep happy. It may look like an average cell phone, but it works worldwide and can't be traced."

"Nice," she said, impressed.

"As far as school goes," he continued, "one of our doctors will call you in with the flu or something. If the CIA can't arrange for you to make up a few missed classes, the free world's in a lot of trouble."

Sydney laughed with relief. "I still have to change my clothes, though. Or is what I'm wearing okay?"

"Not remotely," Wilson said, with an amused shake of his head. "But don't worry, I have you covered."

He motioned to someone outside Op-tech, and an older woman strode in, rolling a large suitcase behind her.

"I think you'll find everything here," she told Wilson, parking the case at his feet.

"The paperwork?" he asked.

"All inside. Good luck," she added, winking at Sydney on her way out.

Wilson heaved the suitcase onto the table and

popped it open. "Looks okay to me," he said, digging through the women's clothing inside. "What do you think, Sydney?"

"Wow."

The clothes were incredible. Designer labels Sydney had only read about in magazines marked the shirts, dresses, and pants that lay folded in neatly organized piles. Prada, Balenciaga, Narciso Rodriguez . . .

She reached out to touch a soft green dress. "This can't all be for me?" she asked, amazed. A few strands from an auburn wig peeked out from the assorted hats, heels (were those *real* Manolo Blahniks?), accessories, and—*yes!*—lingerie.

"Your cover," Wilson explained, removing a manila envelope before snapping the case closed again. "We don't have much time left, so listen closely."

Wilson opened the envelope and started passing her its contents. "You'll be posing as a rich, jet-setting tourist. Here's your plane ticket, passport, and some cash."

He pushed a huge stack of euros toward her, but Sydney reached for the passport instead, opening it curiously. The picture was hers, but the name . . .

"Kate Jones?" she said, looking questioningly at Wilson.

"Your official SD-6 alias." He smiled. "At least until you blow your cover and we have to reestablish you as someone else."

Sydney returned his wry grin. "I guess I'll be Kate for quite a while then."

Wilson chuckled, but the humor drained quickly from his face.

"Confidence is good. Just don't let it get you killed."

* * *

The long black limousine pulled out of the SD-6 garage, merging seamlessly into the light Saturday traffic. From her spacious seat in back, Sydney watched the downtown streets slip past her tinted windows like scenes out of a dream.

This certainly feels like a dream, she thought. In keeping with Sydney's cover, Wilson had ordered the deluxe SD-6 limo, complete with blacked-out windows, satellite television, cut-crystal decanters, and a heavily armed driver separated from the back by an opaque, bulletproof divider. There was so much extra room in the passenger compartment that Sydney's new suitcase lay spread open on the floor, more evidence of a dream. No one who knew her could say the contents of that case had anything to do with her experience of reality so far.

"Change clothes in the limo, and put on some makeup," Wilson had directed, pressing the suitcase's handle into her hand. "Don't forget—you're rich and glamorous now. Make sure you wear that money belt under your clothing at all times, and keep your passport on you, too. In this business, you never know when—or if—you'll see your luggage again."

The limo driver had appeared by then and was waiting outside Op-tech. Sydney had simply nodded, overwhelmed by how quickly things were moving.

"You're staying at the Plaza Athénée," Wilson had continued hurriedly. "It's swanky. You'll like it. Your reservation's under the name Carrie Wainwright."

"What about Kate Jones?" Sydney had objected, confused.

"Kate's just for travel, Sydney. At the hotel, you're Carrie Wainwright."

"Oh."

"And that's all you need to know for now. When you check into your room, you'll be met by the agent in charge of the mission. Do exactly as he says, and you'll be fine."

"How will I recognize him?"

"He'll recognize you. The less you know right now, the better, in case . . ." Wilson had let the sentence trail off uncomfortably. "Just in case."

Sydney had nodded. *In case I get caught.*

"You need to get going now. Oh, wait. One more thing." Taking a small piece of plastic from an inside pocket, Wilson had peeled off a tiny self-adhesive brown dot.

"It's a tracer," he'd explained, reaching to stick the device beneath her collarbone. "Looks exactly like a mole, but now I'll be able to track you until you get there." He'd straightened her collar, then smoothed it down. "Come back safe, okay?"

Sydney had choked up then, and she choked up now, remembering the unexpectedly fatherly gesture. Wilson and the people at SD-6 were becoming like her second family.

Or more like my only family, she thought bitterly.

Instead of trying to fill the aching void of Sydney's mother's death, Jack Bristow had spent the years since the accident driving his daughter as far away as possible. A nanny, an all-girls boarding school, and countless business trips later, Sydney and her father were virtual strangers. She resented him for not wanting her in his life, the same way he seemed to resent the fact that she'd ever been born.

If they didn't actually hate each other, they didn't love each other either. And with every passing year, the gulf between them just grew wider.

The limousine hit a bump, jolting her back to the present.

"Sorry about that," the driver's voice said over the intercom. "LAX in ten."

"What?"

A shocked glance out the window revealed that they were closer to the airport than Sydney had realized. Falling to her knees beside the open suitcase, she pulled out a pink Chanel dress, linen mules, and a matching lightweight sweater and hurriedly began dressing. Yanking the mascara from her new, fully stocked makeup kit, she added two thick layers to her usual light coat and quickly brushed both eyelids and cheekbones with an all-purpose bronzing powder.

If only Francie could see me now! she thought, letting her hair out of its ponytail and completing her new look with red lipstick and movie-star dark glasses. A mirror inside the limo reflected her stylish transformation. *I feel like a model. No, better. I feel like Super Spy!*

One thing was for sure: She didn't look like herself anymore. The knowledge gave her a strange sense of power.

Quickly, confidently, Sydney strapped on the money belt under her dress, loading its hidden pockets with most of her cash. The remaining money, her passport, and her ticket went into a purse that matched her designer suitcase. She'd buy magazines and snacks at the airport, she decided, to look more like a tourist. She even knew which magazines a woman dressed in Chanel would read.

Spying was just acting, really, and she was nothing if not a good actress.

I can do this, she told herself happily, her spirits rising to the challenge. *Whatever happens on this mission, I won't let my country down!*

2

A FLIGHT ATTENDANT'S VOICE came over the big jet's speakers, jolting the passengers to full wakefulness. Unfortunately, he was speaking French.

I should have learned French before Russian, Sydney berated herself, straining to understand him. She was good at languages, but she needed to learn so many for SD-6 that sometimes the prospect of mastering them all made her feel a little desperate. *Not only would French have been easier, I could actually use it right now.*

As it was, she barely understood one French word in ten, and even those she wasn't sure of.

The flight attendant finished his announcement and mercifully repeated it in English: "Ladies and gentlemen, we are on final approach to Orly Airport and will be landing in a few minutes. At this time, please make sure that your seats are in the upright position and that your tray tables are closed and locked."

No problem there, Sydney thought, a bit smugly. SD-6 had sprung for a first-class ticket, partially to support her cover and partially to give her a chance to sleep in the big reclining seat. Between her excitement about her first mission, free movies, and countless cups of coffee, though, she hadn't slept five minutes all night. She had never flown first class before, but it hadn't taken her long to learn that first-class flight attendants didn't let a girl go thirsty or hungry, or do menial things like adjust her own seat back. Even now they were cruising the aisle with hot wet towels, dispensing them with silver tongs.

"Hello, this is your pilot speaking," a new voice said in English. "Paris time this Sunday is 12:22 P.M. The current temperature is eighteen degrees Celsius. We hope you have had a pleasant flight, and that you will keep our airline in mind for your future travel needs. Flight attendants, please prepare for landing."

Sydney craned her neck in a futile attempt to look out the window from her aisle seat. Her stomach told her the plane was descending, but all she could see was sky.

I wish Francie were here, she thought, wanting to share the experience. *I hope she's still speaking to me when I get back!*

She had telephoned her friend before the plane left Los Angeles, full of hastily invented explanations for her sudden departure. Francie had answered the call from her car, already on her way to the beach.

"It's just that the bank needs me to cover for someone in San Diego this weekend," Sydney had lied. "One of their clerks got sick and left them shorthanded."

"And so they need *you*? On a Saturday? To fly to the rescue without even a suitcase? Why can't they cover it with their own people?"

"It's . . . flu. A *lot* of them have the flu."

"Oh, great," Francie had said sarcastically. "Be sure to bring it home and give it to me."

"This is a good opportunity for me, Francie," Sydney had pleaded. "Don't be mad."

"I *am* mad! You promised that if you didn't make it to the beach you'd go to the party tonight."

"I'm sorry. I'll make it up to you."

There had been such a long silence that Sydney

had started to wonder if they'd been disconnected. Then Francie had sighed.

"All right. What's the address?"

"The address of what?"

"Of your hotel room! I hope they put you somewhere good, because I expect a killer pool. They do have a swimming pool, right?"

"You . . . uh . . . you want to come stay with me at the hotel?" Sydney had faltered, mentally kicking herself for not seeing that coming. San Diego was only a two-hour drive from Los Angeles, full of students from three major colleges, and legendary for the bars and clubs just over its border in Tijuana, where the drinking age was eighteen. She and Francie had once driven down and had a great time shopping for cheesy knickknacks and tacos on Avenida Revolución before returning north to roller blade on the Mission Beach boardwalk. Sydney had picked San Diego as an alibi precisely because she knew what it looked like in case Francie started asking questions; she hadn't thought of the now obvious drawback.

"Of course I'm coming!" Francie had said. "We never got to go to SeaWorld last time, so there's your chance to make things right."

"But . . . you can't come," Sydney had blurted out. "I'm going to be working the whole time, catching up on data entry, and I won't be able to go anywhere."

Francie had sighed again. "Well, we can at least go out to dinner. Do a little clubbing . . ."

"I'm going to be working late, and it's only a single room," Sydney had lied desperately. "If they find out you're in there, I might get in trouble."

"For what?" Francie had retorted. "Having a life?"

"I'm sorry. It's just that—"

"No, I'm sorry," Francie had interrupted icily. "Forgive me for thinking you might want my company."

I do want your company, Sydney thought now. *If only the CIA didn't have such strict rules against discussing anything with civilians!*

A flash of color outside the plane window caught Sydney's eye. Buildings came into view. Then pavement. The plane's engines whined. Sydney held her breath, waiting, waiting . . .

Bump! The landing gear hit the tarmac and the plane rolled down the runway.

The pilot's voice came over the intercom again: "*Mesdames et messieurs, bienvenue à Paris.* Ladies and gentlemen, welcome to Paris!"

* * *

Sydney stood in one of the lines to clear airport customs, shifting nervously from foot to foot. So many people had disembarked from various planes at once that the distance between her and the customs inspector seemed to stretch on forever. People with babies and people with baggage, tourists, locals, and would-be immigrants . . . the more people crowding the lines, the more conspicuous Sydney felt standing by herself.

Adjusting her dark glasses, she tried to stop fidgeting—the last thing she wanted was to invite suspicion.

I only wish I knew what was happening to my suitcase while I'm stuck standing here. She pictured it circling around and around, unattended, on the baggage carousel, its showy designer fabric crying out for someone to steal it. *Then what would I do? What would I wear?*

She made herself take a deep, calming breath. The thick bundle of euros Wilson had given her was zipped safely into the money belt around her waist; if she had to, she could buy new clothes. Unfortunately, carrying so much cash was suspicious in itself. She definitely didn't want anyone searching her and finding that kind of money. She shifted her weight, sighed, stood up straight. . . .

The inspector stamped a passport and began grilling the man next in line.

What if my alias doesn't hold up? she wondered worriedly. They had barely looked at her fake passport in the U.S., but this French inspector was giving everyone a hard time. If anyone suspected she wasn't Kate Jones, what would they do to her? Would her mission be over before it got started?

The inspector stamped another passport. Then another. Another. Sydney felt a trickle of sweat run down between her shoulder blades. Finally it was her turn.

The inspector held out his hand for her passport and scrutinized the photograph.

"You are American?" he asked.

"Yes," Sydney replied, grateful that he spoke English.

"Remove your glasses, please."

She pushed her dark glasses up onto her head, trying to appear nonchalant while he studied her face. The effort he was expending on matching her to her photo made her glad she hadn't worn a wig.

"Reason for visiting France?" he asked.

"Vacation."

He cocked a graying brow. "You are meeting someone here?"

Sydney's heart skipped. Had she made a mistake? Was it suspicious to vacation alone?

"Um, yes. A friend," she answered nervously. "She lives here in Paris."

"What is your friend's address?"

"I—I don't have it with me. She's picking me up by car. She's probably waiting outside right now."

The man gave her a probing look. It took every bit of her SD-6 training for Sydney to hold his gaze.

"Length of stay?" he asked at last.

"One week." Wilson had given her a round-trip ticket with the return date a week away. She could exchange it for the real date later, he'd said, but one-way tickets aroused suspicion.

"You have a return plane ticket?"

Sydney nodded with relief.

"Let me see it."

She produced the ticket from her bag, expecting him to inspect it as carefully as everything else. But the man simply glanced at it, then stamped her passport.

"Have a nice stay," he told her. "Next!"

Sydney nearly danced out of the customs area on her way to baggage claim. Her suitcase was on the carousel, no worse for the long delay.

I did it! I'm here! she exulted as she pulled her bag off the conveyor belt. It seemed so easy now, she couldn't believe she had ever been worried.

Finding a direction in which a lot of people were walking, Sydney joined the crowd, her fancy suitcase rolling along behind her. Here in the steadily moving stream, it was no longer obvious she was alone, and even her designer clothes blended in. She was in Paris, after all, fashion capital of the world, and stylish women were everywhere. Sydney picked them out of the throng, strutting in their high heels, speaking in French too rapid for all but a native to understand, greeting their friends with kisses on both cheeks, meeting their lovers with the type of kisses France made famous . . .

The City of Romance, Sydney thought wistfully.

It wasn't as if she didn't *want* a boyfriend. Up until recently, though, the guys she had been interested in had always seemed to find her invisible. Now that they were finally noticing, there wasn't anyone she cared about.

Well, maybe one. But I barely even know Noah Hicks.

Agent Hicks was six or seven years older than Sydney, and far too highly ranked in SD-6 to be interested in a mere trainee. That hadn't kept her from checking him out every chance she got, though. There was something both attractive and rough around the edges to Noah's appearance—the cute guy next door after a few hard knocks—but the pull Sydney felt was caused by something deeper than looks. His attitude was what intrigued her, the way he walked a little taller and moved a little faster than everyone else. Even when he laughed, his intense brown eyes stayed wary. And the first time she'd seen him, in the middle of a Krav Maga training session at SD-6, the precise viciousness of his kicks and jabs had totally mesmerized her.

That's a man, she remembered thinking, *not a college boy*. Even now, walking through Orly Airport, she felt her face heat up.

She had spoken to Noah only once, briefly. Part of the team sent in to extract her when things went bad at the Sandoval concert, he had introduced himself and checked a minor injury to her hands. The most fleeting physical contact—but enough to start her wondering: Was it possible he'd felt something more than professional concern? Now when she walked the halls at SD-6, she was constantly on the lookout for a guy with short, wavy brown hair, a mysterious scar beneath his chin, and an attitude that entered the room before he did.

Reaching the exit at last, Sydney emerged from the terminal and stood blinking in the sunshine of a balmy Paris afternoon. Taxis were lined up waiting for fares, and a man was pointing passengers toward them in order. Sydney headed for the cab he directed her to, grateful when its driver jumped out to help with her luggage.

"Merci beaucoup," she said as he wrestled her suitcase into his trunk.

He smiled and fired off something in French.

"Um . . . the Plaza Athénée?" Sydney replied, hoping he'd asked where she wanted to go.

Her answer obviously pleased him. He chattered away as he opened the passenger door and helped her inside, keeping up the one-sided conversation during the entire time it took him to climb behind the wheel and pull out into traffic.

"Je suis désolé. Je ne parle pas français," Sydney said carefully, offering up her only perfected full sentence along with a sheepish smile.

She had told him she didn't speak French, but the man just laughed and kept talking. Sydney got the feeling he was commenting on the landscape they were passing, but he could have been describing his favorite movie and she wouldn't have known the difference. At first she strained to make sense of the unfamiliar language, but soon she became so caught up in the scene outside the taxi windows that she let the words wash over her just like the warm spring air. She was in Paris, and a man was speaking French to her, and if she didn't understand him, did it really matter? She was just going to drink it in and enjoy the experience.

The highway that had carried them away from the airport soon deposited them on surface streets, which became increasingly mazelike the farther downtown they traveled. Roads never seemed to meet at right angles, and every big intersection was like the hub of a badly mangled wheel. Cars shot in from all directions, then rocketed back out in others, frequently accompanied by squealing tires and honking horns. Paris drivers seemed to know exactly where they were going—and to expect everyone else to get out of their way.

Sydney eventually gave up trying to memorize the complicated route her driver was taking and concentrated on the sights. She had already spotted a cemetery and several parks; now the cab cruised a tree-lined street filled with picturesque shops. Church spires spiked the skyline, reminders of the city's rich history.

I wish we could drive past the Eiffel Tower, she thought, resisting the temptation to ask the driver for a detour. She was supposed to be a rich, worldly tourist; she couldn't continue gawking like a girl straight off the farm. *Maybe I'll see it later,* she consoled herself. *And the Louvre, and the Seine, and Notre Dame . . .*

Or maybe I'll work the entire time and never see anything.

Sydney settled back into her seat, resigned. Whatever Wilson had sent her to Paris to do was more important than sightseeing. Sliding her fingers over her collarbone, she felt her new little mole, reassured by the high-tech bump.

"Voici la Tour Eiffel," the taxi driver announced, pointing through the windshield.

Sydney lunged forward to the edge of her seat. There, far ahead, intricately patterned iron girders stretched up into the sky, capping the city like an exclamation point.

"Now I know I'm really in Paris." She sighed contentedly.

The man laughed and started rattling off what she supposed were facts about the famous landmark. And all the while they drove straight toward it, until its crowning antenna was lost above the car roof and Sydney had to switch her focus to the span of its massive legs instead. Finally the taxi got so close that she rolled her window down and stuck her head outside. Far, far above her the tower loomed, so big it was overwhelming.

Abruptly the cab turned a corner, and almost immediately it turned again, driving out onto a pretty bridge.

"La Seine," the driver said proudly, smiling at Sydney in the rearview mirror. They were suspended over one of the most famous rivers in the world.

The Seine sparkled in the sunshine, more green than blue, its broad expanse alive with colorful boats of all sizes. Its banks were heavily developed with buildings and walkways, but the river still exuded an undeniable charm. Greenery and docks lined its shores as well, and Sydney spotted more bridges both upstream and down.

On the opposite bank of the river, the driver turned again, up another obliquely angled street, and moments later he stopped in front of an impressive-looking hotel. The multistory building was made of honey-colored stone with red fabric awnings at every window. Boxes of red flowers lent additional color to the balconies, and two solid, irregularly shaped domes over the entrance doors reminded Sydney of the separated halves of a giant black-lipped clam.

The driver twisted around in his seat. *"Nous voici! Plaza Athénée!"* he said with a proud wave of his hand.

A hotel doorman was already opening her taxi door, reaching in to help her out. Sydney paid for her ride in a blur as her suitcase was collected and taken into the grand building.

"Merci," she told the driver, adding a generous tip. *"Au revoir."*

The man winked at her as he climbed back into his cab. "Have a good time," he said, driving off.

"He spoke English!" Sydney groaned, realizing too late that he'd been having fun with her. It killed her to think of the information she'd missed on her drive into the city. Maybe, if she'd *asked* him to speak English . . .

From now on, 'Do you speak English?' is the first sentence I learn in every language, she resolved. *And the sooner, the better.*

At the hotel entrance, the doorman was still holding the door open for her. Shaking off her disappointment, Sydney walked beneath the clamshell and into the glass entryway.

The interior of the Plaza Athénée was even more luxurious than the exterior had promised. Sydney caught her breath as she entered the beautiful lobby, feeling like Cinderella at the ball. Surely she couldn't be staying *here*? Wilson hadn't lied when he called the place swanky, but the hotel's glamour went deeper than that. Its very walls seemed to whisper of tradition, and Paris, and haute couture. For a moment she hesitated, feeling like an intruder. Then she threw her head back, adjusted her Chanel sweater, and strode up to the reception desk.

"Hello," she greeted the desk clerk, surprised to hear the slightly imperious tone in her voice. "I have a reservation. Carrie Wainwright."

"Oh, Mrs. Wainwright!" the man responded. "Welcome to Plaza Athénée. I will have the boy show you up to your suite."

Sydney gave the clerk a gracious smile and followed the bellhop, but her mind and heart were both racing as she entered the elevator.

Did that guy just call me Mrs. *Wainwright?*

If Carrie Wainwright was supposed to be married, Wilson might have mentioned it. On the other hand, French was clearly the clerk's first language. He had probably simply misspoken.

That's it, Sydney thought, relieved. *Of course.*

Her heels sank into the carpeting as she exited the elevator and followed the bellhop down a hall, her steps weaving a bit with exhaustion. The twelve-hour flight, nine-hour time change, and complete lack of sleep were beginning to take their toll, and the caffeine and excitement that had kept her awake to that point had suddenly evaporated, leaving her jittery and strung out.

"Voilà." The bellhop stopped in front of a door. Then, to Sydney's surprise, he knocked.

Who does he think is going to let us in?

Her question was answered a second later when a man threw the door open wide.

"Hello, darling!" he said, stepping into the hall to kiss her on both cheeks. "Did you have a nice flight?"

Sydney absorbed his wavy brown hair and intense brown eyes in a state of total shock. "It's you!"

"Of course it's me. Who did you expect? Your *other* husband?" he teased, laughing for the sake of the bellhop.

Handing the bellhop a tip, he hustled Sydney into the room and closed the door behind them. He turned to her expectantly, but all she could do was stare.

"You're surprised," he said at last.

Surprised? Yeah, that scratches the surface.

Her new partner was Noah Hicks.

3

"I HAD THEM BRING up some fruit and sandwiches," Noah said as Sydney wandered past him into the living room. A silver-domed tray waited on the Louis XV coffee table in front of a velvet sofa. "I thought you might be hungry when you got here."

"Maybe later," Sydney said distractedly. Ignoring the food, she made her way to a large, arch-shaped window, pulled aside the long, silky drapes, and looked out over a view that took her breath away. "We can see the Eiffel Tower!"

"Nice, huh?" Noah moved to stand behind her. "We've got the same view from the balcony."

"And this room!" she continued. "Can you even believe this room?"

The walls were painted a warm butter yellow and were hung with original oil paintings. The furniture was eighteenth century, dark wood with gold accents and rich fabrics in blended shades of red, amber, and rose. Silk pillows, patterned carpets, and antique lamps that made Sydney swoon added to the uniquely Parisian ambiance.

"It's not a room, it's a suite," he replied. "Two bathrooms, and wait until you see the marble bathtub. You can have that one."

His offer brought her back to reality.

"Wait. We're *sharing* this room?"

"Suite," Noah corrected. "And I'll sleep on the couch, so don't get the wrong idea. Why don't you sit down and let me explain everything."

Sydney willingly took a plush chair, eager to learn more about her mission.

"As you already discovered," he said, "we're posing as husband and wife. To maintain that cover, we need to be in the same suite, but this is strictly business. You'll have the bedroom, and that door shuts. You don't need to worry about anything unprofessional happening."

Sydney nodded. "Good to know."

At the same time, though, she couldn't help

thinking she wouldn't mind if something a *little* unprofessional happened. *If, say, the future of our country depended on Noah's kissing me, I could probably endure it.*

"Is there a problem?" he asked.

"Huh? No!"

"You have a funny look on your face. Are you feeling all right?"

"Fine."

"It's a long flight. You're probably hungry. Why don't you have a sandwich?"

He seemed so genuinely concerned that she took a crustless triangle from beneath the silver cover. She had already known that Noah Hicks was magnetic, confident, and good at his job; this unexpectedly sweet side only made her like him more.

"You were telling me about our mission," she reminded him between bites.

"Right. Well, if you aren't familiar with Paris, you may not have realized that we're dead at the heart of the fashion district here. SD-6 has intel that one of the newer couture houses, Monique Larousse, may be laundering money for K-Directorate. The house's profits are out of line with sales, and last week a known K-Directorate agent, a nasty piece of work called Alek Anatolii, was seen entering but not leaving."

"What happened to him?" Sydney asked, moving to the edge of her seat. "You don't think . . . you don't think they *killed* him?"

Noah chuckled. "We should be so lucky."

Her expression must have betrayed her shock.

"I'm kidding!" he said quickly. "I mean, sort of. Okay . . . if it wouldn't break my heart, does that make me a bad guy?"

"I'm just surprised to hear you put it like that."

"If you'd met Anatolii, you'd be less surprised. Let's hope he stays missing."

The grim set of Noah's lips made Sydney silently agree.

"In the meantime," Noah continued, "you and I are going to be stepping up the recon on that fashion house, Monique Larousse. So far SD-6 has been surveilling it remotely. Now we need to get inside—and that's where you come in."

"What do you want me to do, Noah?" she asked, totally engrossed.

"For starters, call me Nick. Nick Wainwright. I've been putting it around that I'm a dot-com millionaire from California. And you're Carrie, my spoiled trophy wife."

"Nice," she said sarcastically.

"It's only a cover. Besides, there are worse things than being the wife of a millionaire. Didn't I just fly you out to Paris to buy you a whole new wardrobe?"

"Do I get to keep the clothes?"

He smiled at how fast she saw through him. "Unlikely. But tomorrow morning we have an appointment at Monique Larousse anyway. They'll show you their designs and fit you—and the more time it takes, the better. We're really there to case the place, and plant as many bugs and cameras as we can. Most of that's going to fall on you, since you'll have better access. I'll be waiting wherever the bored husbands sit, in case you need some backup."

"Backup?" she repeated apprehensively. "What kind of backup do you think I'll need?"

"Probably none. I've never seen anyone less suspicious-looking than you. Add that to how young you are and this is going to be a slam dunk. Straight recon, no problems."

She smiled, although she could have done without the reference to her age. The fact that she was younger than Noah was something she'd rather he forgot.

"So I'm actually going to be trying on clothes?"

"Definitely. Make them bring you everything they have. Then you want to see what you're wearing in a different mirror, you want to see it in different light, you want to use the bathroom, you want to see where they sew the clothes, you want to know what's in that cute little room around the corner. . . . Are you getting my drift?"

"I'm taking a tour of the building, whether they want me to or not."

"That's my girl," Noah said, with a conspiratorial wink. Standing up, he retrieved a black canvas bag from the floor near the sofa. "I have something for you."

Removing a jewelry box, he flipped it open, revealing an absurdly expensive necklace on a bedding of midnight blue velvet. A network of diamonds dripped from fine platinum chains, their irregular sizes and heights like a snippet of starry sky.

"For me?" Sydney gasped, overwhelmed. She and Noah barely knew each other, and *this* . . . Her heart was racing so fast she could barely breathe.

"Like it?" he asked with a devastating grin. "Here, let me."

He already had the clasp open. Before Sydney could form a thought, he was leaning over her chair, reaching the ends of the chain around her neck.

"You might want to move your hair," he said.

Obediently, Sydney gathered her loose long

hair away from her neck. The way Noah was bending over her, her face was half buried in his shirt. She could smell the soap he'd used radiating from his warm skin. . . .

"Perfect!" he declared, stepping back. "That's the best-looking transmitter I've ever seen."

"Transmitter?" Sydney repeated weakly.

"Our guy Graham's a genius. A little silver, a little cubic zirconia, and there you go. Looks real, doesn't it?"

"Um, yeah." The necklace was only spy gear.

Which of course I knew, Sydney told herself quickly. *Duh!*

"Graham's the best," Noah continued obliviously. "If I hadn't seen you before, for instance, I would never guess that this mole's fake."

In one quick motion, he peeled it off like an old Band-Aid.

"Hey, Wilson put that there!" she protested, trying to grab his hand. "It's a tracer."

"I know what it is. And you don't need it anymore. Wilson knows you're here now, and as long as you are, you answer to me. The last thing we need is someone else picking up your signal and tracking our every move."

"Oh." She hadn't thought of that.

"I'll go flush it." Noah started to leave the

room, then turned back. "Do you want something else to eat? Because you can always call room service. Have them send up hot fudge sundaes and caviar, or whatever gives you a thrill. The more we spend, the better we look."

Sydney managed to smile, but the long trip had finally caught up with her. "I wouldn't mind if they brought up some aspirin."

Returning quickly to his black bag, Noah tossed her a plastic bottle. "Headache, huh?" he sympathized. "I'm not surprised. Did you sleep on the plane?"

"Not really."

"I never do, either. Sleeping in public . . . not the safest idea in our line of work."

"Right." Another thing she hadn't thought of.

"If you're not hungry, why not go to bed?" he suggested. "It wouldn't hurt to rest up for tomorrow. The bedroom's all yours—just unpack and make yourself comfortable."

"I don't need to go to *bed*," Sydney protested. It wasn't even dinnertime yet, and still quite light outside. "I'll just take a couple of aspirin, and maybe lie down for a few minutes. I guess I'm kind of jetlagged."

"Take your time. I'm not going anywhere." Noah held up her fake mole. "Except off to flush.

Let Wilson track the sewers awhile," he added with a grin.

"He wouldn't really—" she began anxiously.

"Not for more than five minutes. Will you relax? I'm running things now."

Sydney watched him disappear, then got up and dragged her rolling suitcase into the hotel bedroom, closing the door behind her. The case seemed heavier now than it had in L.A., the locking catch almost too complicated for her fumbling fingers. She got it unlatched at last, and began hanging up her expensive new dresses to avoid any further wrinkles. What didn't need hanging got left on the floor, the idea of tackling a strange dresser suddenly too overwhelming.

I'll do it later, she thought, falling across the sumptuous bed. The upholstery and linens in the bedroom were as rich as in the rest of the suite, but Sydney was too exhausted to notice. Even the cut orchids on her nightstand barely registered. *My poor pounding head! What did I do with those aspirin?*

She knew she should get up to look, but her body seemed to have already melded to the mattress. Besides, what she really wanted to do was call Francie. Her new cell phone still bulged in her sweater pocket. Wrestling it out, Sydney flipped the instrument open and contemplated its black buttons.

There has to be some sort of generic version of all this that's okay to tell her, she thought. She hated keeping her friend in the dark, especially when she was so used to sharing every little detail. She wanted to tell Francie about SD-6, and Wilson, and Paris, and the real reason she took off running every time her "bank" pager beeped. Most of all, she wanted to tell her about Noah.

Maybe I can just say there's a coworker on this business trip who's kind of cute. That seems normal enough. Non-CIA people get crushes. Except . . . what time is it in L.A.?

In Sydney's jet-lagged state, the simple math required to figure out the time difference seemed nearly impossible. She decided to try anyway.

If the flight from Los Angeles to Paris takes twelve hours, and Paris clocks are nine hours ahead . . . No, wait. It doesn't matter how long the flight takes. I just have to subtract nine from whatever time it is now. Except that it's only three or four o'clock here, and that makes a negative number. Wait, I've got it. First I have to add twelve to get military time. And then I have to subtract . . .

She fell asleep still clutching the phone.

SYDNEY AWOKE WITH A start. The room was dark, and for a moment she didn't know where she was. Then she remembered and sat up abruptly.

A soft hotel blanket fell away from her chest, pooling at her waist. Her legs were still covered, but she could feel that her feet were bare. Someone had come in while she was asleep to take off her shoes and cover her up.

There was only one person that someone could be.

How embarrassing! she thought. And a moment later: *How sweet!*

The fact that Noah had been able to get that close without waking her didn't make her look like much of a spy. But the fact that he'd wanted to . . . What did that mean?

Swinging her bare feet down to the plush carpeting, Sydney rose and switched on a lamp. A previously unnoticed clock by the bedside indicated that it was 6:04 A.M. She had slept through the whole night.

Great.

She imagined Noah hanging around the evening before, waiting to see if she'd wake up for dinner. *I hope I wasn't snoring when he came to check on me!*

She paced her room, wondering what to do now. There was no sound coming from outside her door. Noah was probably asleep on the couch, and she didn't want to wake him. Now that she was up, though, her excitement at being in Paris had come rushing back full flood. Going back to bed was not an option; she could barely even stand still.

I'll go for a run, she decided. A jog through the Paris streets would let her see more of the city, and the cold dawn air would be perfect for clearing the remaining cobwebs from her head.

Taking a T-shirt and designer tracksuit from her open suitcase, Sydney dressed quickly. SD-6 had thought of everything, right down to running shoes and the fancy chronometer she strapped to her wrist. Grabbing a fabric bag of toiletries, Sydney went into the adjoining bathroom to brush her teeth and hair, creating a high ponytail. She opened her bedroom door slowly, to make sure there were no squeaky hinges, and slipped silently into the living room.

On the sofa, Noah was wrapped haphazardly in a blanket, his face dimly lit by the predawn light coming through a crack between the curtains. He looked so cute and helpless—younger than when awake, despite his stubbly cheeks—that Sydney stopped to stare in wonder. She never would have imagined that Noah could look so completely peaceful.

For a moment, she considered touching him, just to prove that she could sneak up on him too. Her hand stretched out and hovered an inch from his thick brown hair. She could almost feel her fingers buried there, stroking the stray strands away from his warm forehead. . . .

What would he do if he woke up? she wondered. She imagined him smiling, happy to see her. Then she imagined him breaking her forearm in one swift motion, her bones snapping like dry twigs before he was fully awake.

Given his training, the second possibility seemed more likely. But even if he didn't hurt her, there was no good reason to assume he'd enjoy waking up to find her fingers in his hair. What if things got awkward because he didn't understand why she'd touched him?

What if they got awkward because he did?

Sydney lowered her hand and stepped away, more afraid of revealing her budding feelings than of having her arm broken. She could say it was all a game, that she was only getting him back for sneaking up on her, but then she'd sound like a child. She could never tell the truth and admit that she'd been longing to touch him since the moment they met . . . because what if he didn't feel the same way?

If there's going to be anything between us, he's going to have to start it, she decided reluctantly. *I just can't hang myself out on that limb.*

Tiptoeing to a table beside the door, Sydney found two hotel key cards and some touristy maps of Paris. She took a key and slipped the smallest folding map into her pocket.

Then, with one last look back at Noah, she stole silently out of the room.

* * *

On the pavement outside her hotel, Sydney took a deep breath of the early-morning air, feeling it tingle through her body. In the quiet half-light of dawn, Paris seemed to belong just to her, and she was ready to run out and greet it. Turning left on impulse, she began jogging up the street.

Avenue Montaigne turned out to be a treasure. Right there, in just a few blocks, some of the most famous fashion houses in the world rubbed stony shoulders with Sydney's hotel. She kept a tally as she ran, going up one side of the street, then down the other: Christian Dior, Nina Ricci, Chanel, and—barely a block past the Plaza Athénée in the other direction—the darkened Théâtre des Champs-Élysées.

She wished she could attend a play in Paris or, better still, see an opera. Maybe, if they had time, she could talk Noah into going. If SD-6 had outfitted him as thoroughly as they had her, he couldn't pretend he had nothing to wear.

Making a left toward the river, Sydney visualized Noah in a tuxedo. He would look handsome, she decided. Sophisticated. Her feet hit the pavement, step after step, but her mind was far away.

I wonder if he's interested in me at all, she mused as she turned left again and began running along the Seine. *Or if he ever could be.*

Was the fact that they were in Paris together just a coincidence?

Or was it fate?

She was about a kilometer from the hotel when

she came to a bridge and had to make a decision: Go right, over the Seine, or turn left and stay closer to home? Stopping to pull the map from her pocket, she took a moment to figure out where she was. The bridge she was standing next to was called the Pont des Invalides. As tempting as it was to run over the Seine, there were a couple of big palaces on her route if she turned left. She decided to check out the palaces. Then, all of a sudden, she noticed something else: In the spokelike network of streets between her and the Plaza Athénée, someone had drawn a small blue dot and neatly printed *ML*.

Monique Larousse, she thought with a rush of excitement. *That's got to be it!*

She had known they were staying close to the couture house, but she hadn't realized how close. *I could run over there and check things out before Noah even gets up.*

She liked the idea of doing a little reconnaissance on her own, just to get a feel for the place. The couture house wouldn't be open yet, but she didn't plan to go in anyway—she just wanted to see what the outside of the building looked like. Maybe she'd notice something that would prove useful later.

Making a diagonal left away from the river, Sydney ran briskly through the quiet neighborhood, looking for her target. Moments later, she spotted it up ahead.

Monique Larousse was not quite as upscale as some of the other couture houses, but it was doing well enough to occupy a three-story building in a long row of attached structures. The storefront was painted beige, its ground floor dominated by large display windows emblazoned with the initials *ML* entwined in gold script. The windows were sheltered by dark green awnings, their color repeated in the painted wood trim.

Sydney jogged past slowly, trying to catch a peek through the darkened windows before crossing the street and jogging back in the other direction. The sun was just beginning to come up, washing the street in a rosy glow. Everything seemed peaceful. Nothing about the building looked the least bit suspicious.

Which is the look I'd be going for too, if I were breaking the law, Sydney thought, determined to learn something. Running to the street corner, she discovered a narrow alley extending behind the fashion house, separating its row of buildings from a similar row facing the next street. She turned and began trotting up the alley, still searching for any clue.

Dumpsters were spaced out along its length,

and one was located directly across the pavement from the back of Monique Larousse. Behind the Dumpster, the bushy, overgrown ground rose at an incline until it encountered the back walls of the buildings in the next row.

Sydney jogged past the rear of the fashion house, imagining emergency scenarios. The Dumpster and bushes afforded some cover, but not much. The back of Monique Larousse was beige and nondescript, with a steel door at the bottom of an exterior staircase that descended to basement level. Sydney had just slowed her steps, trying to memorize everything, when all of a sudden she heard a car engine coming toward her down the alley. The motor seemed loud in that echoing space; the vehicle was moving quickly. Acting on instinct, she ran the few steps to the Dumpster and ducked behind it, planning to hide until the vehicle went past.

Except that it didn't. A decrepit black van stopped just feet away and two men hopped out onto the pavement.

Sydney watched them from her cover, careful not to make a sound and alert them to her presence. Barely breathing, she spied as one of the men opened the double doors at the back of the van, unloaded a long parcel wrapped in black plastic, and carried it down the stairs to the basement door. She was dying to know what was in the package, but there was no way to sneak past the huge second man, who had lit a cigarette and was now smoking it near the van's driver-side door. He wore a gray beret pulled forward on his otherwise bald head, and his shoulders were so broad that even the unhealthy gut straining his shirt buttons didn't make him look less formidable.

A minute later, the first man reappeared. The driver flicked his cigarette onto the pavement and the duo climbed into their van and drove away. Sydney crept cautiously out of hiding, wondering what it all meant.

It doesn't have to mean anything, she reminded herself, trying to look casual as she strolled toward the basement stairs. *A place like this probably gets lots of deliveries.*

But at sunrise? Besides, the men must have had their own key, since nothing was leaning against the basement door now.

I'll tell Noah what I saw, in case it's important, she decided, beginning to run back toward the hotel. *If nothing else, he ought to be impressed by my initiative!*

* * *

"You did *what*?" Noah demanded, furious. "I *know* I couldn't have heard you right the first time."

"I just thought . . . ," Sydney offered lamely. "I mean, since I was there . . ."

"Do I have to remind you who's in charge of this mission?" The sweet, sleepy look of that morning had vanished, replaced by one of pure belligerence. "Are you crazy?"

"I only wanted to help," she protested, wishing she'd kept running instead of returning to the suite. She had been so eager to tell Noah what she'd seen. Obviously that had been a mistake.

"I will not have you freelancing on my assignment!" he said, punching the back of the sofa for emphasis. "Did you ever stop to think that there might be security cameras on that building? You may have already blown our cover!"

"No way!" she said quickly. "If anyone saw me, I just looked like a jogger."

"A jogger who hides behind Dumpsters," he said derisively.

Sydney pressed her lips together to keep them from quivering. She could feel her eyes filling with tears, and if even one escaped, she was going to feel more stupid than she already did. She shifted back and forth in her jogging shoes, pulling her jacket tightly around her and wishing she were anywhere else.

"I see your point," she admitted. "But even if someone saw that, it doesn't prove I'm not some clothes-crazy American tourist, spying on my favorite designer. Or maybe I'm just afraid of running into someone alone in an alley. A lot of women are."

Noah gave her a disgusted look. "You shouldn't even talk to me right now. Go take a shower or something."

She hesitated, torn. The way Noah was behaving made her want to get as far from him as possible. But how could she leave things like this between them?

"I'm sorry if I made a mistake," she said, trying to hold his angry stare and finding it impossible. "I'm trying my best, but I'm still a trainee."

"You don't have to tell me *that,*" he retorted. "Believe me, it's incredibly obvious."

Sydney nodded miserably, the aching lump in her throat like a fist squeezing off her voice. Without another word, she turned and ran for her bathroom, slamming two doors behind her.

Stripping off her running clothes, she lurched into the shower and turned on the pressure full blast. The hot, cleansing water poured down on her head, but it couldn't wash away Noah's harsh words. Her tears broke like a storm, shaking her whole body.

Everyone else at SD-6 always told her how great

she was doing, and she had believed them. Except for that immersion tank fiasco, she had received top marks in every training session. But training was training, and this mission with Noah was the real thing.

What if she couldn't cut it?

Wilson only picked me for this because I can wear the clothes, she told herself. Maybe that was all she had to offer. Maybe no one even expected her to do more.

No one except Noah.

He was so mean! she thought, a new set of sobs convulsing her. *Why did he have to be so nasty?*

Instead of sneering at her for being a trainee, shouldn't he be cutting her some slack? He must have been a trainee himself once—although maybe he liked to forget that.

He's a self-righteous jerk, she decided resentfully. *I don't know why I ever liked him in the first place.*

One thing was certain: She didn't like him anymore.

He had yelled at her, embarrassed her, made her cry, and—worst of all—made her doubt herself.

Noah Hicks isn't so crushworthy after all.

* * *

"There you are!" Noah said cheerfully when Sydney finally reentered the living room.

She had taken her time in the bathroom, drying her hair, putting on makeup, and trying on every one of the outfits SD-6 had sent with her. She'd checked them all in the full-length mirror before deciding on a dress to wear later that morning to her appointment at Monique Larousse. She'd selected a layered auburn wig as well—just in case she *had* shown up on a security camera.

Back in control of her emotions at last, and unable to delay any longer, Sydney had thrown on some jeans and reluctantly emerged to face Noah. Now she viewed him with studied coolness, a slight shrug her only reply.

"I ordered us some breakfast," he said, gesturing to a room-service cart by the window. Crystal, silver, cut flowers, and white linen made the meal look extra special, and the number of dishes, both covered and uncovered, indicated the extent to which he had over-ordered. "I, uh, I didn't know what you'd want, so I just got everything."

"Why not?" she said sullenly. "It isn't your money."

To her surprise, he winced. Hurrying over to pull out a chair, he motioned her toward it hopefully.

"Look. I might have overreacted earlier," he

said. "I mean, not about what you did. But I could have explained it nicer. I'm sorry I lost my temper."

"Don't worry about it."

The last thing she had expected was an apology, and it was amazing how little it helped. Raising her chin a notch, Sydney took the chair he offered—not because she forgave him, but because no matter how she felt, Noah was still in charge of the mission.

He dropped into the seat opposite her. "You have to try these croissants," he said eagerly, passing her a plate. "I had one yesterday, and they practically melt in your mouth."

Sydney put a croissant on her plate, merely following orders. Noah beamed. It was harder to stay mad when he smiled like that, but she was completely determined.

"Anything else I need to know before we leave for Monique Larousse?" she asked, using the twin excuses of butter and jam to avoid looking at his face.

"There's some technical stuff, some gear to go over. But we've got plenty of time. Try the coffee—it's fantastic."

He reached across the table to fill her cup himself, swearing when he sloshed some over the rim into her saucer.

"Oops," he added sheepishly. "Sorry."

Sydney pressed her lips together—this time to

keep from smiling. It was of absolutely no importance that they were having the most romantic breakfast ever, in full view of the Eiffel Tower. Or that Noah was clearly anxious to smooth things over. Or even that he appeared to be genuinely sorry. She saw through his boyish charm routine. She wouldn't let him under her skin a second time. At least, not any farther under.

"What kind of gear?" she asked.

"Bugs, cameras, an earpiece to go with that necklace transmitter. The usual. You've probably seen it all before."

"I probably have," she agreed. "I may be a trainee, but I'm not untrained."

Noah gestured to the cart. "Have some eggs."

Breakfast progressed as awkwardly as it had begun. Sydney helped herself to some of everything, determined to be at peak strength for their mission. Noah made sporadic attempts at conversation, most of which she quashed with one reply.

Eventually he fell silent, leaving her to battle a growing sense that she was behaving worse than he had. Even so, she refused to give in. All her life, she'd been vulnerable. She hated it—the sick, sneaking suspicion that any second someone would pull security out from under her like a magician's tablecloth. Whether or not he realized it, that was exactly what Noah had done.

"I'm full," she announced at last, pushing away from the table. "When are we leaving?"

Noah checked his watch. "Not for another two hours. I hired a limo to drive us there—it might look strange if we walk."

"I'll take my time getting dressed, then. If I meet you out here in an hour, does that give us time to go over the gear?"

"Plenty of time."

"All right. See you then."

She started to head for the bedroom, but Noah stood up abruptly, blocking her way.

"Sydney . . . are we okay?"

"What do you mean?"

"I mean you and I. We have to work together here. And we didn't get off to a very good start."

"We're fine."

His eyes searched hers. "You seem upset."

"I'm not. Why should I be?"

"You shouldn't." He touched her wrist uncertainly, the warmth of his hand shooting straight to her heart. "Are you?"

"No."

"You probably think I was too hard on you." He shrugged. "Maybe I was. But you're not the only one with something to prove on this mission. I'm in charge, you understand? If we fail, I have more to lose than you do."

"You're in charge. I understand perfectly."

He seemed unconvinced. "So we're okay?" he asked at last.

"I said we were."

"No hard feelings?"

She forced a smile. "I'm not a child."

But the words she spoke didn't match the decision she'd come to: *I'll follow his instructions to the letter. I'll do my job like a pro. And then, if I'm lucky, I'll never see Noah Hicks again.*

A guy like Noah could break a girl's heart.

5

THE LIMOUSINE PULLED TO the curb in front of Monique Larousse, Sydney and Noah sequestered in back. Sydney had thought it ridiculous to hire a car for such a short distance, but with the heels she was wearing, she had to admit it was easier than walking. Besides, Noah had ordered the limo, and she wasn't about to second-guess him out loud.

The driver turned off the engine and hurried around to help Sydney out. She gave him her hand, painfully aware of the shortness of her skirt as she attempted to exit the car gracefully. Keeping her knees together, balancing on the chauffeur's gloved hand, she finally managed to get one spiked heel on the curb and leverage her weight up over it—not an easy trick.

They spend so much time on weapons training at SD-6, she thought, embarrassed. *They ought to have a class on high heels.*

Because, unlike earlier that morning, the street was alive with people. Locals and tourists both cruised the storefronts, browsing for bargains or simply window-shopping. And, unless Sydney was mistaken, a disproportionate number of them were suddenly staring at her.

It's probably the limo, she thought self-consciously.

But as Noah walked around the car to join her, Sydney caught her reflection in Monique Larousse's plate glass windows. She had seen herself in the mirror back at the hotel, but at the time she'd been so consumed by details that she hadn't really *seen*. She had checked to make sure her wig was straight, her lipstick even, and her bra straps covered by her sleeveless blue silk sheath, but all of a sudden, out here on the street, she barely recognized herself. Her three-inch heels and short dress made her legs seem impossibly long, the layered russet wig was straight from *Charlie's Angels,* and most shocking of all was the haughty look on her well-made-up face.

Who *was* that rich snob? No wonder people were staring.

Noah told the driver to wait. Then he turned to Sydney. "Are you ready to do this?" he asked.

"Let's go," she said tensely.

She watched her reflection stride toward the green door as if she were watching a stranger. Where had that walk—no, that *strut*—come from? Was it only her lingering annoyance with Noah putting that attitude into her step? Or had she tapped into something deeper, something she hadn't even known she possessed?

The door to the couture house opened abruptly, an older man inside falling all over himself in his haste to welcome her.

"Bonjour! Bonjour, madame," he said, bowing as he waved her inside. *"Bienvenue à Monique Larousse."*

"Why, thank you. Aren't you sweet?"

Her voice didn't sound normal either, but the look in the man's eyes was pure admiration. Something clicked in Sydney's brain: Whatever Noah thought, Wilson had been right to choose her. Her confidence came flooding back, along with renewed excitement at embarking on her first mission. She'd show Noah a thing or two.

"You must be Mr. and Mrs. Wainwright," the man said, switching to English.

"Call me Nick." Noah slung a possessive arm across Sydney's shoulders. "We've come to buy the better half here a new wardrobe."

"Of course, of course. Please come in. May I offer you a glass of champagne?"

"Sounds good to me!" Noah boomed, turning heads. "I don't suppose you have satellite TV?" He laughed at his own joke, totally transformed into the nouveau-riche dot-commer he had come there to portray. "You know women," he added, with an indulgent pinch of Sydney's cheek. "Better bring the bottle."

"Whatever you like, *monsieur*—er, Nick." The man gestured for them to walk ahead of him. "But first, if you'll please choose a seat . . ."

The interior of Monique Larousse looked more like a huge formal living room than a store. The walls were papered in an antique floral pattern, the ceiling was intricately plastered, and the overhead light came from chandeliers. Several groupings of antique furniture were arranged on rich rugs, with not a rack of clothing in sight. Monique Larousse sold only custom and one-of-a-kind designs, and only by appointment; browsers seeking sales were in the wrong place.

Five other customers, a couple and a group of three women, were seated near the far end of the room, being catered to by saleswomen. As Sydney watched, three models wearing summer suits and hats came through a curtained doorway and stood before the women.

Noah selected a place to sit near the center of the store, a spot with good visibility in all directions. Their attendant disappeared to fetch the champagne while Sydney perched on the edge of a striped silk chair.

"So, here we are," she said, trying not to sound nervous.

Noah stretched back in a settee, his hands locked comfortably behind his neck. "Here we are," he agreed.

She glanced around her, wondering what to do first. In a row across the inside of her left palm, five surveillance cameras—flesh-colored lumps the size of half a pea, with adhesive on the back—waited to be transferred to strategic areas of the building. The clutch purse in her lap contained a box of bugging devices disguised as tiny breath mints. But now didn't seem like the moment to break any of those things out. Instead, she fidgeted with her necklace, trying to feel the stone that held the transmitter.

She and Noah had practiced in the hotel before they'd left—all she had to do was whisper and he heard her in his earpiece. She had a duplicate earpiece, like a miniature hearing aid, which received Noah's voice from a transmitter in his top shirt button.

Sydney's hand drifted up to her earlobe as she pretended to adjust an earring that was actually another camera. In less than a second, she'd snapped several pictures of the room, not knowing what might be useful. Then it occurred to her to focus on the employees, any or all of whom could be working for K-Directorate.

Keeping her movements casual, Sydney snagged shots of all three models, the two saleswomen, and a thirty-something woman who had appeared through a distant doorway. Her flawless skin was the color of milk, her hair an unnatural black, and her lipstick neon red. She watched the models a moment, scowling, then disappeared again just as the doorman reemerged with a tray of champagne and hors d'oeuvres, a smiling young saleswoman in tow.

"I am Yvette," the woman announced as the champagne and food were offered. Sydney took a flute of champagne but declined the hors d'oeuvres, while Noah filled a napkin with crab puffs as if oblivious to the fact that the tray was about to be set down right beside him.

"Thank you, Henri," Yvette told the man. "You may go now."

Henri bowed slightly before disappearing into the back of the shop, giving Sydney the perfect opportunity to catch both him and Yvette with a single shot of her earring cam.

"So! What are we looking at today?" Yvette asked cheerfully. "Daywear? Eveningwear? Perhaps a peek at our fall collection?"

"Daywear. *And* eveningwear," Sydney added quickly. Noah had said to make things take as long as possible.

Yvette ran off and Sydney sipped her champagne. The wine tasted nearly as bitter as the unexpected memory it provoked. She remembered the first time she'd had champagne, at a cold Christmas dinner with her father—his closed-off, brooding face, her desperate need to impress him with how much she'd matured at boarding school. She had badgered him until he'd let her have the drink, so even after she'd discovered she didn't like it, she'd had to finish it all, afraid of looking foolish. It hadn't mattered to him, of course. She understood that now.

"Penny for your thoughts," Noah said.

She managed a noncommittal smile and put her champagne down on the table, grateful to see Yvette reapproaching with two models in evening dresses.

For the next forty minutes, Sydney and Noah watched as store models paraded back and forth wearing Monique Larousse originals. Sydney was overwhelmed, both by the outré fashions and by the mere idea of what they must cost. She pointed at items on impulse, knowing none of the clothes would be hers anyway. Eventually Yvette decided it was time to move on to a fitting.

"We will get your measurements, then perhaps you would like to try on some of the samples, just to get a feeling," she said. "Of course, anything you select will be made to order."

"How long is that going to take?" Noah asked. "We're only here for a week, and we want to bring these clothes back to the states with us."

Yvette looked surprised but recovered quickly. "That might be possible. For some of the gowns. If we alter the samples."

Noah nodded. "That's what I like to hear, Yvette. Think outside the box."

The saleswoman smiled uncertainly and whisked Sydney off through a wide doorway. On its other side, a long hall extended to the left and right. Yvette turned left. Following her, Sydney glimpsed two well-furnished, bedroom-sized rooms through open doorways before Yvette stopped in front of a third.

“We will be in here,” she said, motioning Sydney inside. “Madame Monique prefers that we fill the other rooms first—she thinks they are better decorated—but I favor this one because it is largest. It’s nice, don’t you think? Look, your choices are already here.”

Sydney walked in, noticing that opposite the dressing room doorway the hall took a ninety-degree turn toward the back of the building. Unfortunately, a dividing curtain across the second hallway kept Sydney from seeing more, and Yvette quickly shut the dressing room door.

The room they were in seemed much like the others Sydney had glimpsed. One wall was completely mirrored, and several freestanding mirrors were placed about to allow viewing from all angles. The other three walls were paneled with wood, and the floor was wood as well, enhanced by a colorful area rug. A tall bureau, several white brocade chairs, and a loaded chrome clothes rack accounted for the rest of the furniture in the room.

“First, I will take your measurements,” Yvette announced, removing a measuring tape from the bureau’s top drawer.

Over the next few minutes, Sydney submitted to an intricate series of measurements, keeping her left hand curled to conceal the cameras and trying not to betray her increasing impatience.

She'll get the measurements, then she'll leave so I can try on the clothes, she reassured herself. *That will be my chance to do a little exploring.*

But when Yvette attempted to unzip Sydney's sheath, Sydney realized that wasn't going to happen. The woman planned to stay and dress her like a doll.

"You know what? I can do this by myself," she said, twisting away from Yvette's fingers. "In fact, I'd prefer to. I'll call you if I need help."

"Madame Monique will not like that," Yvette said uncertainly. "I am supposed to assist the customer at all times."

"How about assisting my husband for a while, then? He's probably totally bored out there."

"Oh. Well . . . if you wish, I'll go see."

"Thanks. I won't be long," Sydney promised, shooing the woman out the door.

She was finally alone in Monique Larousse.

"Noah! Noah!" Sydney whispered, kicking off her spike heels. "Yvette's coming your way. Can you hear me?"

He coughed—their signal for yes.

"Keep her busy."

Sydney opened her purse and took out her

packet of "breath mints." Trying to move casually in case she was under surveillance, she pretended to put a mint in her mouth but actually dropped the chalky white bug behind one of the white chair cushions.

"Have you got her?" she whispered, barely moving her lips. "I'm going out."

"Hey, Yvette, what's the verdict?" Noah's voice came back in her ear. "Did Carrie already buy up the shop?"

Yvette's answer was crystal clear; she had to be standing nearby. "She is, um . . ."

"Listen, these crab cakes are great. Where do you buy these?"

"I do not know. Let me ask Henri."

Sydney was already reaching for the doorknob when she heard something she hadn't expected: Noah speaking French.

"Vous êtes très aimable," he said. *"Merci beaucoup."*

"Vous parlez français!" Yvette cried delightedly.

"Pas très bien. Je prends des leçons depuis une année maintenant. J'ai appris les verbes importants et la plupart des animaux de ferme."

Yvette giggled.

One hand on the doorknob, Sydney nearly

burst out laughing as well. She had no clue what Noah was saying, but she'd heard enough French to realize how painfully American his accent was. It gave her a perverse sort of pleasure to know that Mr. Perfect had a weakness after all.

Yvette's voice grew flirtatious. *"Vous parlez très bien, monsieur."*

Noah's rambling reply was punctuated by more giggles from Yvette, and Sydney felt an unexpected pang. Even with his lousy accent, she had to admit that Noah's French sounded kind of romantic.

Yvette obviously thought so.

For a moment, Sydney wanted to march out to the front of the store and break things up.

Which would mean I was jealous, which would mean . . . Get a grip, Sydney, she thought, annoyed with herself. *I told him to stall Yvette, and he is. Besides, even if he's totally hitting on her—*

"I'm going in," she whispered abruptly, opening the dressing room door.

Noah interrupted his conversation long enough to clear his throat.

Her heart fluttering with adrenaline, her purse in her left hand and bugs in her right, Sydney slipped barefoot into the hall.

6

JUST OUTSIDE HER DRESSING room door, at the corner where the hall changed direction, Sydney peeled a camera off her hand and, pretending simply to brush against the wall, stuck it to the wallpaper. The paper's busy floral pattern and a special coating on the camera made the device virtually disappear.

That's one, she thought, breathing fast with excitement and a little fear. Even though the mission was a simple recon, with Noah right outside, she couldn't stop imagining someone from K-Directorate watching her at that very instant. Taking a deep breath, she continued nervously forward, ducking around the dividing drape in the second hallway.

The change in décor was immediate. While the front of the store was all opulence and antiques, the hallway behind the curtain was strictly utilitarian. Plain white walls, industrial gray carpeting, and overhead fluorescent lights made a charmless combination. The only grace note was a large window at the end of the hallway, clearly original to the old building. Walking quickly to the window, Sydney leaned on the sill and looked out, letting a bug tumble into a crack in the wood there while she was at it.

Outside, a familiar alley greeted her eyes; she was gazing through one of the ground-level windows she had passed on her jog that morning. On the other side of the pavement, the Dumpster cast a block of shade onto the bushy ground behind it. And to her right was the exterior staircase that led to the basement door, where the mysterious men in the van had dropped off their parcel that morning.

If I could just get down a floor and over a bit, she thought, *I could see where they came in. Maybe I could even find that package.*

Pushing off from the window, she looked around as if lost, then opened the nearest door. As she had hoped, a staircase lay on its other side.

Sydney's heart was beating double-time as she

padded down the stairs, planting another camera halfway to the bottom. She was far from the dressing room now, and every step she took was putting her more at risk. The sound of Noah's voice, still nattering on in French, was her lifeline now. She had long since quit trying to understand what he said, but his calm, steady tone emboldened her to keep going.

At the bottom of the stairs, a doorway opened into a short, grubby hallway lined on both sides with closed wooden doors. Sydney recognized the single steel door at its end as the exit to the outdoor stairway.

That's where those men came in! she thought excitedly. She quickly placed a camera in the hallway, where it would film any further deliveries, and dropped a bug into the crack between the filthy carpet and baseboard.

Now, where would that package be?

If she could find it and prove it was something important, Noah would have to admit that her unauthorized snooping that morning had been pretty smart after all. The problem was, she didn't know which door to look behind, and she could hardly run around opening them at random—someone might be behind one.

She was still trying to work out a plan when she

heard heavy steps clomping down the stairs outside. Somebody was coming!

With no time left to be cautious, Sydney yanked open the nearest door and dodged inside, closing it behind her just as two men entered the hallway. She could hear their muffled voices from the dark, windowless office where she found herself.

That was close, she thought, pulse pounding. Pressing her ear to the door, she listened to the men talk in the hall, but couldn't make out what they said. Her just-placed bug and camera would catch everything, though, and she felt kind of proud of how skillfully she'd managed the situation. All she had to do now was wait for the hallway to clear.

Which hopefully won't take long. There has to be a limit to how long Noah can charm Yvette.

Not that he seems to be reaching it.

He was still chatting and Yvette was still giggling, their voices crystal clear in Sydney's hidden earpiece. *If he weren't supposed to be married to me, he'd probably have asked her out by now!*

Meanwhile, the two men were still yakking in the hall, keeping her trapped. Sydney glanced back into the small, dark office, then decided to search it more thoroughly. Taking a tiny flashlight from her purse, she shone it around the room.

An old wooden desk and two cobweb-covered bookcases were the primary furniture, and judging from the layer of dust covering everything, they didn't get used very often. Sydney eased a couple of desk drawers open, but found nothing more exciting than pens. The mysterious package of that morning was nowhere in sight, nor was there anyplace to hide something that big. She dropped a bug into the crack between the bookcases and returned to listen at the door.

The men were *still* out there, still talking, when all of a sudden a different voice rose in Sydney's ear—Noah's. Speaking English.

"She's not in the dressing room?" he said loudly.

Sydney's heart vaulted into her throat. They'd noticed she was missing!

"But Madame Monique," Yvette protested, "I just left her there."

"Then I suggest you find her," a sour third voice replied. "Now."

"Nothing to get in a panic about." Noah spoke as if he were cautioning Sydney directly. "Knowing my wife and her peanut bladder, she's probably in the bathroom."

Sydney strained against the closed door. Noah's message was clear: She had to get back upstairs fast and pretend to have needed the toilet. But the men were still in the hallway, and there was no way to get past them.

"So, you're Monique Larousse," Noah continued conversationally. "My wife sure likes your clothes."

"Thank you. That's very flattering," the third voice replied stiffly.

"I'll go look in the ladies' room," Yvette said nervously.

The next second there was silence.

Are they still there? Sydney wondered frantically. *Did I lose my transmission?*

She adjusted her earpiece, but still heard nothing.

Suddenly, Noah cleared his throat. "So . . . here I am, all by myself," he muttered lightly, as if simply uncomfortable at being left alone.

Sydney felt sick. He wanted her to know that he'd lost sight of both Yvette and Madame Monique. They could be anywhere, and they were looking for her. She had to get out of there!

But the men were still talking . . . talking . . . talking. . . .

Sydney was ready to scream when the voices suddenly stopped. She heard the sound of heavy boots, followed by a slamming door. Silence.

A few more seconds: still no sound.

Yes! she thought gratefully.

She bolted out of her hiding place—only to come face to face with the huge bald man she'd seen driving the van that morning.

He had stayed behind to smoke in the hall. Now a barely lit cigarette dangled, forgotten, from his thick fingers. He stared at Sydney, as shocked as she.

And then the expression on his coarse face turned into something less pleasant.

"Que faîtes-vous ici?" he barked, dropping his cigarette on the carpet.

His eyes smoldering like its embers, he started walking toward her.

7

SYDNEY NEARLY PANICKED AS the heavy-set man came toward her. She tried to remember her Krav Maga training, but everything she'd learned swirled through her brain in a frightened blur. Could she really defend herself hand to hand against an opponent so much bigger? Her instincts told her to bolt into the alley and run for her life.

But running will prove I'm guilty, she thought. *And leave Noah and SD-6 exposed.*

She had to try to bluff.

"Finally!" she exclaimed huffily, walking forward to meet her assailant. "I was starting to think no one worked down here!"

The man's steps faltered in confusion.

"Do you speak English? My husband speaks French, but he's upstairs and I'm hopeless with languages."

"I speak English," the man admitted cautiously.

"Great! Fantastic! What's your name?"

"Arnaud."

"Arnaud—Isn't that pretty? Pretty in a manly way, of course. I'm Carrie Wainwright."

Her mind was working so fast, she felt dizzy. She had thrown him off for the moment, but Arnaud looked like the kind of guy who'd only put up with so much small talk. She needed a story and she needed one now. Casting about for inspiration, her gaze fell on his still-burning cigarette.

"Do you have any matches?" she asked.

He looked at her strangely. "Matches?"

"I was just going to sneak out back here and have a cigarette. I would have gone out front, but my husband's in the showroom and he thinks he's the nicotine police, I swear. Don't you hate it when people hassle you about smoking?"

Arnaud's lips hesitated on the verge of a smile. And then he remembered something.

"What were you doing in that room?" he asked accusingly.

"I told you. Looking for matches." She let her tone get a little offended. "I didn't touch anything, if that's what you're worried about."

"We'll see," he said, striding past her into the office.

For a moment she was alone in the hallway. Instinct took hold of her again, insisting that she run. She had a clear shot at both stairways now. . . .

"All right," Arnaud said, reemerging. "I see you are telling the truth."

Sydney's legs almost buckled with relief.

The man fished in his pocket. "Here. Use my lighter," he offered, flicking it into flame. "I'll light your cigarette for you."

"Aren't you sweet?" she murmured, nearly passing out.

He had just hit on the flaw in her little cover story: She didn't have any cigarettes.

Arnaud stood looking at her expectantly, his lighter still at the ready. Sydney began rummaging through her purse, hoping for a miracle. She didn't smoke, but SD-6 seemed to have packed everything else. . . .

Except cigarettes.

"I can't believe this," she said desperately. "I

had them when I left the hotel. I must have lost them in the limo."

Looking up, she dared to meet his eyes, only to find him smiling at last.

"I hate it when I lose them," he said. "Here. Have one of mine."

"Thank you!" she exclaimed.

Taking the cigarette he offered, she put it in her mouth and leaned over his lighter, hoping she wouldn't choke. Except for a couple of rebellious attempts at boarding school, she had never smoked at all. She hated the smell of cigarettes, and the cancer part was a big minus too.

She had just succeeded in lighting up when Yvette came barreling down the stairs. Exhaling quickly, Sydney put the cigarette behind her back, pretending fear of being caught.

"Vous voilà!" Yvette exclaimed. "What are you doing down here?"

"I, uh . . . I was just looking for the bathroom?" Sydney said, intentionally unconvincing.

Arnaud snickered. Sydney nudged him in the side, managing to pass her cigarette to him behind her back.

Yvette sniffed the air, not fooled.

Summoning up her most winning smile, Sydney appealed to the saleswoman. "We don't need to tell my husband about this, do we? It would be worth an awful lot to me. In fact, I feel a real shopping frenzy coming on."

Yvette laughed. "Your husband believes you are in the bathroom," she reported with a conspiratorial wink. "He implies you spend much time there. Something tells me this is not the first time you have used this excuse, *oui*?"

Sydney shrugged, still working the smile. "There are some things a man doesn't need to know."

"I agree. But since he knows you are missing now, perhaps we should go back upstairs?"

"Lead the way," Sydney told her, amazed that she'd pulled it all off. "See you around, Arnaud!"

The big man tipped his beret at her, an amused grin on his face.

* * *

Nearly two more hours elapsed before Sydney and Noah collapsed into the safety of their waiting limousine.

"I think that went well, don't you?" Sydney asked the moment the driver left the curb. She had tried on countless samples and lost track of the outfits she'd ordered, but the most important thing was that she'd distributed all of SD-6's bugs and cameras without arousing suspicion.

"As long as you got what you want, I'm happy," Noah said.

"What do you mean what *I* want?" she protested.

His knee nudged her sharply, his gaze shifting meaningfully from her to the driver. The glass divider was up, but Noah obviously didn't want to take a chance on being overheard.

"That, uh, that red dress was all for you," she covered.

He smiled. "I'll have to admire it *later.*"

Later, right. I get the picture, she thought sarcastically.

But she wasn't mad at Noah anymore. How could she be, after what they'd just been through together? Aside from that one close call with Arnaud, everything had gone perfectly, and Sydney was still buzzing from the adrenaline rush of danger and success.

"I'm going to call my friend Francie," she announced, taking her cell phone from her purse.

Noah cocked an eyebrow at her, but she ignored him. She was dying to talk to someone, and she couldn't tell Francie anything it wouldn't be safe for the chauffeur to overhear anyway.

Dialing quickly, Sydney waited for ages before Francie finally picked up.

"Hello?"

"Francie! Hi! It's me."

"Sydney?" Francie said groggily. "What's the matter? Is something wrong?"

Sydney caught her breath as she realized her mistake.

What time is it in L.A.?

"No! Nothing," she replied, doing frantic math in her head. *Add the twelve, subtract the nine . . .* "What makes you say that?"

"Oh, I don't know. Maybe the fact that it's still dark outside." Francie sounded more awake, but not especially happy about it.

"You're kidding! It is?" Sydney covered the phone with one hand while she pretended to go check. *Let's see, that would make it . . . just after four in the morning there.*

She waited a few more seconds, then took her hand off the phone. "Francie! I'm so sorry. The clock in my room is wrong, and with the blackout drapes and everything, I didn't even notice. I just wanted to say hi before you left for class."

"What are you talking about? Aren't you coming home today?"

"I wish I could, but I'm really busy here."

"So now you're missing school? You're insane. I don't know why you work for those people."

"I know. Listen, how was the Delt party? Did you go?"

"It was okay. I didn't meet any interesting guys, but some other girls from our floor were there, and we danced until two in the morning. The band was the best part, and they're playing at the Lion's Den next weekend. If you can tear yourself away from the bank."

"We should go," Sydney said. "We will."

"Don't say it unless you mean it."

"We'll *try,*" she qualified hurriedly.

She wasn't even positive she'd be back home by the weekend. The first stage of the recon was over, but she had an appointment with Yvette on Wednesday to try on some of the clothes she had ordered. Was Noah going to expect her to stay?

"You sound like my mother," Francie grumbled.

"I do? Well, then, eat your vegetables, I guess. Do your homework, and I'll see you when I get back." She managed to get off the phone without Francie asking her exactly when that would be, but just barely.

"Still working out the kinks with the time change, huh?" Noah said, amused.

"No," she replied, not about to admit her mistake to him. "Everything worked perfectly."

Besides, even if she'd had to lie about her reason for waking Francie up—and pretty much everything else—it had been worth those few moments of panic just to hear her friend's familiar, grounding voice.

The limo pulled up outside the hotel, and Sydney could barely keep from opening the door herself in her excitement to get upstairs and rehash the mission with Noah. Somehow she restrained herself long enough to wait for the chauffeur, but by the time she and Noah stepped out of the elevator on their floor, she was positively bursting.

He'll have to admit I did a great job now, she thought, trailing him down the hallway. Their door came into sight. Suddenly Noah stopped short.

"I had the Do Not Disturb sign out. Did you move it?" he asked.

His voice was so low and intense that Sydney froze in her tracks.

"No," she whispered, peering at the doorknob over his shoulder. There was nothing hanging there now.

"Do you have your key?" he asked.

Sydney produced it from her purse and held it out to him, but Noah shook his head.

"Stand to the side of the door, and open it on my signal," he directed, pointing her into position. Then he reached under his jacket and pulled out a gun.

Sydney took her place, wondering if her eyes were as wide as they felt. She hadn't even known Noah was armed.

He gestured for her to use the key: "Ready . . . set . . . *now!*"

Sydney threw the door open and Noah burst inside, his gun leading his body. She held her breath, waiting for the ensuing firefight.

Nothing happened.

Daring to peek around the open doorway, Sydney saw Noah in the living room, still in a shooting stance. But his only opponent was a newly cleaned room, complete with fresh flowers and fruit.

"It was only the maid!" she exclaimed, laughing.

Noah spun around, his expression warning her back to silence. Moving cautiously, he crept out of view in the direction of the bedroom and bathrooms. Sydney remained paralyzed, not daring even to breathe until Noah reappeared and put his gun back in its holster.

"Nobody's here," she concluded, walking inside and closing the door behind her.

But again he shook his head, holding a finger to his lips.

Reaching into a jacket pocket, Noah produced what appeared to be a silver fountain pen. She watched as he removed the cap, then unscrewed the nib as well. From inside the case, where the ink should have been, he removed a long, slender instrument capped by a tiny red light. The light was blinking.

Sydney looked at him questioningly.

"Come out on the balcony," he said calmly, slipping the instrument into his pocket. "I want to show you something."

He opened the balcony door and stepped outside, motioning for her to follow. Sydney joined him silently, not sure what was going on. Noah shut the door firmly behind them.

"Pretty, huh?" he said, turning to gesture toward the Eiffel Tower. "The air is so clear today."

Sydney gave him a disbelieving look. He had brought her outside for *that*?

"Romantic, don't you think?"

Her disbelief turned to shock.

"There's something I have to tell you."

His gaze locked with hers, and suddenly Sydney felt breathless. They had never stood quite so close before. She saw flecks of amber in Noah's brown eyes. If she lifted her hand, she'd be able to trace the scar beneath his chin.

"What is it?" Her voice came out a whisper. The way he was looking at her . . .

And then, just as she'd known he would, Noah reached out and took her into his arms. She stiffened as he pulled her tight to his body, but the way his lips brushed against her ear did strange things to her pulse.

"Can you hear me?" he breathed, so low it was almost like hearing his thoughts. His breath was warm against her neck. His mouth nuzzled her ear. Her heart pounded out of control as his hand ran up into her auburn wig.

"Yes," she forced out somehow.

He pulled her even closer. "Our room's bugged. Somebody's made us."

8

"CAN I SAY SOMETHING now?" Sydney asked.

Noah finally nodded, allowing her to blurt out the question that had been tormenting her for the past hour.

"Noah, what are we going to do?"

They were standing beside the Trocadéro Fountains, a long, shallow pool filled with sequencing fountains directly across the Seine from the Eiffel Tower. Between the splashing from various vertical jets of water and occasional lengthwise volleys from the powerful water cannons at one end, the noise would cover their conversation.

“Well, first of all, try taking a breath,” he said. “Are you feeling okay?”

Sydney nodded, but his question made her realize how stressed out she must look. From the moment they’d discovered their suite had been bugged until just then, when they’d arrived on foot at the fountains, everything that had happened had passed in an anxious haze.

Per Noah’s whispered instructions, they had both showered and changed every article of clothing they’d worn to the couture house, in case they’d picked up a listening device there. Sydney had ditched her wig as well, dressing quickly in a loose printed dress with a sweater tied across her bare shoulders, her money, passport, and phone secreted in the pockets of the hidden belt around her waist. Dark glasses, a wide-brimmed hat, and flat sandals completed her touristy ensemble. She had seriously considered wearing her running shoes instead, in case of a fast getaway, but had reluctantly decided the look wasn’t stylish enough for Carrie Wainwright—assuming anyone still believed that was her name.

“Rule number one: We stay calm,” Noah said now, keeping his voice low despite the splashing fountains. “We got this far in one piece, so they must not be sure about us. My guess is that right now we’re only under suspicion.”

"But how?" Sydney asked. "What did we do wrong?"

Noah shrugged. "Most of the time you never find out. Something put somebody's radar up. Maybe finding you downstairs?"

"No way. I totally covered that," Sydney insisted. "Yvette and Arnaud were both convinced I went down there to smoke."

"Right. And you weren't lying to them, so they *couldn't* have been lying to you."

"Noah," she said, a terrible new thought occurring to her. "That K-Directorate agent who disappeared . . . you said he was a big guy, right?"

"Anatolii? Yeah."

"Bald, with a huge gut?"

"Blond. And more like the Terminator. Why? What are you thinking?"

"Arnaud. But no."

"I heard his voice over your transmitter, remember? That wasn't Anatolii."

"Oh. Besides, he and Yvette are both really nice. I don't think they could have anything to do with K-Directorate."

Noah laughed, a short, humorless bark. "You think you can rule people out as agents just because they're nice? How about you? Are you nice?"

She didn't answer, embarrassed.

"Listen. If you want to stay alive in this game—and I'm starting to think I'd like that a lot—don't trust people because they're nice. Nice doesn't mean squat, understand? Meanwhile, a total jerk might risk everything for you. You have to learn to see past that stuff."

She nodded, instinctively knowing he spoke the truth. And had he just said he'd like her to stay alive?

Well, obviously he doesn't want me killed. We're on the same side.

But his tone had seemed to imply something more. Something personal. She was dying to ask what he'd meant . . . except that then he might think she cared.

"So what do we do now?" she asked instead.

"We stick to our cover. We're here as tourists—we act like tourists. Maybe we can throw them off by playing our roles perfectly. We're just Nick and Carrie Wainwright, young marrieds with too much money."

"But we can't even talk in the hotel," she protested.

"No. And I'm not completely sure that there aren't cameras in that suite too. Or, if there aren't, that there won't be by the time we get back. The less time we spend at the hotel now, the better."

"I agree."

"I have an errand later, but I'll take you with me. You've got your passport?"

"Yes. Have you?"

Noah put his hand to his abdomen, indicating that he, too, wore a money belt beneath his button-down and khakis. A blazer hid his gun. "Always. That and cash are your tickets out."

"My plane ticket!" she groaned, remembering. "I should have brought that too."

"Well, it's not important—as long as you have money."

"Wilson gave me half a bank. It's making my waist sweat."

"Good." He smiled. "That's very good."

An unwelcome thought struck her. "You're not sending me home today?"

"Not yet. If you bail before that appointment on Wednesday, it will look suspicious now. I just want to be sure we can get out of here fast if we need to. Call it paranoia." He shrugged. "Or call it experience. In the meantime, we're just sight-seeing fools in Paris. Is there anything you'd like to do?"

Sydney immediately pointed across the Seine to the Eiffel Tower. It loomed over the river, dominating the view. "I want to go to the top."

Noah laughed. "You really *are* a tourist, aren't you?"

"You asked," she reminded him defensively.

"Okay, Mrs. Wainwright," he teased, giving her shoulder a gentle push. "Your wish is my command."

* * *

"Too bad the restaurant isn't serving now," Noah said. He and Sydney were riding a crowded double-decker elevator up from the second level of the Eiffel Tower, where the closed restaurant was located. "I've heard it's excellent."

"I'm sorry we missed it," Sydney replied, but only to be polite. Who wanted to waste time eating when the entire city of Paris was stretching out beneath their feet?

"No, you aren't."

She couldn't help smiling at his cute, sulky expression. "If it doesn't break my heart, does that make me a bad person?"

"It makes you a lousy gourmet."

"I can live with that. Besides, I'd much rather get up to the viewing platform."

"Well, you're *finally* getting your way," he said, making his point about the length of time they'd had to wait for one of the yellow elevators. Tourists had flocked to the famous monument that Monday, eager to see the view from the top in such exceptional weather.

"And it was worth it," Sydney rejoined. "I can see for miles from right here."

But the view through the windows of the packed elevator was nothing compared to the sight that greeted them when they got out. The third-level viewing gallery was almost nine hundred feet above the city, and wide open to the clear blue sky. A mild spring breeze ruffled Sydney's hair as she dashed from point to point along the sun-warmed metal railing, trying to absorb the city from all four sides. Paris spread beneath her like a gift, more beautiful than she had imagined. She felt like throwing her arms open wide and shouting to the tiny mortals below.

Noah wove his way through the crowd to reappear at her side. "Like it, huh?"

"It's . . . amazing," she finally answered. "Completely incredible."

"We can probably spare enough change for the telescope," he teased. "They say that on a day like this you can see for forty miles."

Sydney gazed through the powerful blue telescope, thrilled when she identified the Arc de

Triomphe all by herself. Noah stood close by, pointing out the massively domed Sacré Coeur church and other famous sights, his shoulder grazing hers as she twisted the telescope back and forth. He seemed to know everything about the city—landmarks, street names, history. Sydney found herself getting lost in his voice, surprised by how safe she felt. With Noah at her side and tourists all around her, it was amazingly easy to forget the reason they'd fled the hotel.

"What do you say we get down from here and find someplace else to eat?" Noah asked when she'd completely exhausted the view.

"Are you still hungry?" she asked guiltily, having forgotten Noah's disappointment over missing the tower's restaurant.

"You ought to be hungry too," he said. "If you're not, eat anyway."

She saw the sense in his argument. With everything about their mission suddenly up in the air, they might need the strength later.

"You know where I'd love to eat?" she asked. "At one of those sidewalk cafés, the kind you see in the movies."

Noah smiled, and for a moment she thought he was going to accuse her of extreme tourism again. But all he said was, "We can probably manage that."

The café they found a few blocks away was exactly what Sydney had dreamed of, with cloth-covered tables arranged on the wide, tree-lined sidewalk and crowds of people strolling by. Waiters in white aprons bustled back and forth, bringing sandwiches and salads and bottomless cups of café au lait.

"I was hungrier than I thought," Sydney admitted, polishing off her last bite of *tarte tatin,* a sort of upside-down apple pie.

"Me too." Noah checked his watch. "We still have some time to kill. Do you want to see the Louvre?"

"Are you kidding me? Yes!"

They paid their bill, Noah's ridiculously accented French coming in useful once again, then hired a cab for the short ride to the famous art museum.

"All this is the Louvre?" Sydney exclaimed as they got out of the car. "It's huge!"

Noah grinned. "Don't expect to see it all today." And then he reached out and took her hand.

Sydney tensed with surprise. A deep breath later, she allowed her hand to relax into his. After all, they were supposed to be a married couple—he was just making it look real.

Anyway, it's not like holding hands with Noah

is torture, she thought as they walked toward the center of the enormous U-shaped museum compound. *He may be a brutal boss, but he's still a pretty good guy.*

Besides, the more she got to know him, the more certain she became that life had kicked Noah around some. She didn't know how, and she didn't know why. She just felt it in him somehow—that still-raw wound buried down at his core. If they ever learned to trust each other, they'd have a lot to talk about.

Without realizing what she was doing, she squeezed Noah's hand. He squeezed back. Her eyes snapped to his as she jolted back into the present. Had she given her feelings away?

But Noah simply smiled, not making anything of it.

Why would he? she thought, relieved. Noah was worldly, experienced—not a bit like the immature college boys she'd met so far. Holding hands was no big deal to a guy like him. To her, on the other hand . . .

The entrance to the Louvre was through a large, modern glass pyramid in the center of a courtyard surrounded by sixteenth- and seventeenth-century stone buildings. The glass-walled structure seemed both overlarge and out of place, an iceberg in the warm waters of the neighborhood wading pool.

"This pyramid . . . ," she said tentatively as Noah led her inside it. "It's kind of . . . new."

"You're not the only one who thinks so," he told her. "There was a huge stink when they built this thing."

"Is it permanent?"

Noah gave her an ironic half-grin. "Nothing's permanent. So what do you want to see first? How about the Mona Lisa, tourist girl?"

Sydney removed her sunglasses and perched them on the brim of her hat. "Lead the way," she said eagerly.

For the next couple of hours they toured the art museum's collection of famous sculpture and paintings: da Vinci, Michelangelo, the Dutch masters, Goya, and so many different French painters that their names all blurred together. Sydney saw medieval and Egyptian antiquities, artifacts from Greece and Rome, antique furniture and jewelry, and even the underground foundation of a medieval French fortress that had been leveled hundred of years before to make way for other buildings at the site.

"You're right. We're never going to see it all today," she told Noah at last. "I'm getting vertigo."

"But how are your feet holding up?" he asked. "That's what really matters."

"Are we walking somewhere else?"

"Come on," he said. "I'll show you."

Outside the art museum, the late afternoon air had cooled noticeably. Sydney untied her sweater from around her shoulders and pulled it on as she and Noah strolled through the formal garden in front of the Louvre, crossed the street, and found themselves in an even bigger one.

"This is the Jardin des Tuileries," Noah informed her. "Something else on every tourist's must-see list. You're just checking off the sights today."

He was making fun of her again, but Sydney not only didn't care, she slipped her hand back into his as they walked up the wide central boulevard bisecting the formal gardens.

In front of them, three fountains played in three separate round pools, and to their left flowed the Seine, tranquil and green in the afternoon light. Sydney and Noah walked on without talking, just one contented couple amid so many others. When they came to a big fountain in their path, Noah put his arm around her to guide her in his direction. Far from tensing up this time, Sydney leaned against him as if they were truly in love. It all seemed so perfectly natural, she almost forgot they were spies.

Eventually they skirted a second fountain as well,

but Sydney's attention was already focused ahead, on a massive stone needle pointing straight to the sky.

"What is that?" she asked, turning her body closer to Noah's as she pointed.

"An Egyptian obelisk. We're going to walk right past it."

"You know this whole city, don't you?" she blurted out, curiosity finally getting the better of her. "How many times have you been here?"

"A few," he said with a shrug. His expression didn't invite further questions, and Sydney didn't ask.

They had to cross a busy street to get to the obelisk, but when they finally stood at its base, Sydney stared up in awe. The tapering four-sided needle from Luxor was covered with hieroglyphics cut three thousand years before. Towering over the Place de la Concorde, the square where it stood, it seemed, like so much of Paris, a few degrees larger than life.

"Everything's special here," she sighed as she and Noah continued on their way. "The entire place is magic."

"Let's hope so," Noah said with a wink.

She smiled uncertainly, unsure what he meant. *He's probably talking about the mission. A little luck wouldn't hurt right now.*

But the way he'd been escorting her around all

afternoon, doing whatever she wanted, acting as if he genuinely liked her . . .

All this peace and love is only our cover, she reminded herself. *Don't make anything of it.*

But still . . .

"The Champs-Élysées," Noah announced as they entered a broad, tree-lined street. "Are your feet sore yet?"

"They're fine," she lied, wishing she'd worn her running shoes.

L'avenue des Champs-Élysées, the most famous street in Paris, was known for its width, for its origin at the Arc de Triomphe, and, perhaps most of all, for its shopping. Sydney and Noah walked awhile longer, past palaces and gardens thick with trees, before arriving at a huge, multispoked intersection and, ultimately, the shopping district.

On the section of street before them, life seemed to spill out of the buildings onto the broad pedestrian walkway. Cafés placed their tables in the thick of things, letting foot traffic flow around them. People dined and shopped, or greeted friends and gawked at the sights. Some were there just to be seen, dressed to a degree that would be absurd in L.A. but seemed just right in Paris.

"Wow," said Sydney.

Noah put his arm around her again as they

wove down the crowded pavement, evidently pleased with her response. "Not bad, huh? I've always liked it here."

She still wanted to grill him on the subject of how many times he'd been to Paris, and why, and for how long, but she restrained herself somehow. For one thing, he obviously didn't want to talk about it. For another, she wasn't sure she and Noah were up to the personal questions stage yet.

And when we are, I'll probably start with that scar, she decided, sneaking a sideways glance at his face. Noah's profile was blunt, his nose and chin both rounded, and there, under his jawline, snaked the scar that intrigued her so much. *I'll bet he got it on a mission.*

It gave her a thrill to imagine, although she hoped she wouldn't end up with a similar souvenir. On Noah, it looked good—visible proof that he'd been through something dangerous and come out on the other side. It made her feel safer to know that he could fight his way out of a corner.

"Here we are," he said abruptly, steering her hard to the left, toward the front of a small but ritzy antique shop. "I need to stop in here a minute."

His arm slid off her shoulders, leaving her to follow him in or not. Sydney wandered in behind him, entranced by the items for sale all around her.

From what she could see of the inventory, the shop specialized in antique writing desks and pens. Noah had already reached the counter in the back, where he stood waiting to speak to the clerk, but Sydney walked slowly through the displays, enchanted by both the standing writing tables and the ingenious folding lap desks full of drawers and compartments for parchment, quills, and sealing wax. She ran her fingers over an especially beautiful rosewood box, admiring the burnished brass hardware and wishing she could buy it as a keepsake of her first real mission.

The clerk put down the telephone and greeted Noah in French.

"Yes, hello. I'm Nick Wainwright," Noah responded in a low voice. "You have an item I special ordered?"

"Ah, Mr. Wainwright!" the clerk replied. "It is here."

The man bustled off and returned seconds later with a large square box, already gift-wrapped, in a fancy paper shopping bag.

Sydney moved closer to the counter just in time to see Noah take out a huge wad of cash and pass it to the man uncounted. The clerk smiled and pocketed the money. No one mentioned a receipt.

As Noah turned to leave the store, Sydney fell into step behind him.

"What's in the box?" she asked eagerly.

He flashed her an exasperated look, but recovered his cool quickly.

"That's for me to know and you to find out," he teased in his fake-husband voice. "Maybe it's for your birthday."

9

NIGHT WAS FALLING AS Sydney and Noah exited the taxi that had carried them back to the Seine. Lights sparkled on the river, a thousand tiny reflections from the buildings, bridges, docks, and numerous boats that still cruised the dark waters. Most of the vessels were large and crowded with tourists on sightseeing trips, but Sydney also saw a commercial barge and some smaller, faster craft, which she assumed belonged to local pleasure seekers.

Noah motioned for her to follow him down a dock to the water's edge.

"Come on," he said. "We're taking a boat trip."

"From here?"

The dock Noah had chosen was neither crowded nor well lit, and only a few small boats had tied up alongside it. "All the big tourist boats are over there," she added, pointing across the river.

"We're looking for something a little more . . . private," he told her impatiently. Turning away, he walked hurriedly down the dock, his large paper shopping bag knocking against his leg with each stride, and Sydney had to rush to catch up.

From the moment they'd collected his package at the antique shop, Noah's attitude had changed. He was tense again, impatient, brusque—the guy she hadn't much liked that morning. But this time she realized something: His attitude wasn't aimed at her, it was all about the mission. Once Noah's mind was on the job, there didn't seem to be room for anything else.

Noah stopped at the first boat where someone was visible on board and barked out a question in French. The man paused in the middle of polishing a hatch, staring as if Sydney and Noah were crazy. Then he shook his head and waved them away. Noah continued down the dock, undeterred.

"What did you say to him?" Sydney asked, trotting to keep up, but Noah just kept walking.

At the very end of the dock, a gray cabin

cruiser bobbed in the wakes from passing boats, the peeling paint on its hulls a remnant of happier days. A man reclined in a folding chair on its deck, drinking wine straight from the bottle.

"Bonsoir!" Noah called to him. *"Ça va?"*

The man peered at them through the gathering darkness, then rose unsteadily to his feet. His clothes were torn and filthy, and a dark wet stain spread across the front of his shirt.

"He's drunk," Sydney whispered, disgusted.

Noah smiled without humor. "And poor. Two points for us." Leaving Sydney on the dock, he jumped aboard and began a conversation.

Whatever Noah was saying, the man seemed to like it. He interrupted and protested a lot, but his eyes had begun to glitter with ill-concealed hope. Moments later, Noah took a wad of bills from his pocket and pressed them into the man's hand. The old wino glanced at the money, then tried to exit the boat so quickly he almost fell into the Seine. He passed Sydney on the dock, his odor overwhelming.

"Bonsoir," he said with a leering wink before he stumbled off into the night.

"Come on. Get in," Noah said urgently, offering Sydney his hand.

She grabbed it and climbed aboard. "What did you do? Buy the boat?"

"Let's just say that if he finds it back here tomorrow, he'll consider it a bonus."

"But we are bringing it back. Right?"

"Don't know yet. How are you at steering one of these things?"

"You're not serious."

He gave her another of his I'm-on-a-mission looks. For everyday things like meals and sightseeing, Noah was charming and relaxed. But when it came to his job, he was wound tighter than a French knot.

"You are serious," she declared, resigned. "Fine. Show me how to start the engine."

Sydney's experience with boats was limited to rowboats, canoes, and a single day of speedboat training with SD-6. But the Seine was a big river, and Noah had rented what looked like a pretty slow boat.

Once I get it pointed in the right direction, how much can really go wrong? she reassured herself.

Noah started the cranky engine, then went below with his package. Sydney heard him rummaging around in the dark, swearing under his breath, while she stowed loose items up above. She would be steering from the deck, looking forward over the low roof of the boat, and she didn't want any old wine bottles rolling under her feet.

"I can only imagine what it smells like down there," she called to Noah through the gangway hatch.

A light finally switched on and Noah appeared at the base of the short ladder. "You don't want to know. So are we out of here or what?"

Sydney crossed her fingers. "I'm ready if you are."

Together they cast off the dock lines, and Sydney steered the boat into the river. Noah relaxed visibly as they left the shore, leaning against the outside of the cabin.

"You don't have to take us all the way out to the middle," he said. "Stay to the right and just crawl along. We're not in a hurry anymore."

"Why are we on a boat?" Sydney finally dared to ask.

"That package we picked up is the monitoring device for the bugs and cameras you planted. Everything they've recorded since we left Monique Larousse is waiting to be downloaded, and I need a safe place to do it. Somewhere we won't be disturbed. Or watched."

He glanced up and down the river. Full darkness had fallen, and there were no other boats nearby.

"This ought to be all right. Except for the

smell," he added. "By the time I'm done down there, I'll need to burn these clothes."

Sydney smiled. "Poor Noah."

"Whatever. Listen, don't get too far from the shore, but don't get too close, either. I don't want anyone sneaking up on us that way. Keep your eye out for anything and everything, understand?"

"I will." Her grip on the wheel was still white-knuckled, but she was growing more confident by the second.

"All right. I'm going to set up below. Call me if you see *anything*."

"Don't worry."

By the dim light Noah had on in the cabin, Sydney could now peek through the gangway to see him clearing a small central table of countless nights of takeout, old rotting food in soggy containers. She nearly gagged just imagining the odor, but Noah was undeterred, throwing everything into the boat's little sink. He pushed a pile of dirty clothes off the adjacent bench onto the floor and sat down to open his box.

The monitoring device he removed looked like a laptop with a pair of large padded headphones. Putting the phones on, Noah hunched over the glowing computer screen and started typing. She could see his profile, but not the monitor, and soon she gave up trying. Whatever he was doing, he would probably be at it a long time. Meanwhile, she had a boat to steer.

She drifted down the river, her eyes scanning for anything unusual. At night on the Seine it wasn't hard to see why Paris was called the City of Light. The buildings onshore were giddy with light, and tourist boats carried floodlights to illuminate anything that wasn't already blazing like a Christmas tree. Red and green running lights twinkled on smaller boats like Sydney's, and every bit of brilliance was reflected by the smooth black water. It felt peaceful, just drifting, breathing in the cool night air.

Until Sydney came to an unexpected fork in the river.

"Noah!" she called, not sure what to do.

He jerked upright so fast he bumped his head on the cabin's low ceiling. "What's happening?"

"There's a fork coming up. Which way should I go?"

He was ready to run to the rescue, but when he heard the problem he groaned with annoyance. "You gave me a heart attack for that?" he complained. "I don't care. Make an executive decision."

She nodded and steered to the right. Noah returned to his monitor.

"Finding anything good?" she asked before he could put the headphones back on.

"Not yet. I pulled down the shots off your earring cam—the salespeople and Monique Larousse—and sent them to SD-6 to see if they can match anyone up with our file of known agents."

"Monique Larousse? But I never saw her."

"Black-haired babe? *Night of the Living Dead* skin?"

"*That's* who that was?" she asked, remembering the scowling woman she had spotted so briefly.

"A couple of the stationary cameras you planted aren't working," Noah continued.

"What do you mean they aren't working?" she cried. "I put them up the right way!"

"You probably did. But this technology isn't bullet-proof. You get a camera that small . . ." He shrugged. "Sometimes they break. Sometimes they get knocked down. And sometimes there's interference."

"What kind of interference?"

"Just let me get this done, all right? And then I'll tell you everything." The headphones went back over his ears and Noah was lost in his mission again.

A large tourist boat had begun to overtake them. Sydney steered closer to shore to let it pass. The boat was a good distance out in front of her when all of a sudden it swept its floodlight up and to the left, over the spires of a grand cathedral. Sydney caught her breath in awe.

"Notre-Dame," drifted back to her from the boat's P.A. system, but she didn't need to be told. The ancient cathedral was an incredible sight in the floodlight's ghostly round beam, looming larger as she drifted nearer. She imagined the countless poor laborers working with their crude tools, devoting their lives to a dream they would never see finished. That generations of faith and backbreaking toil could accomplish such staggering beauty was inspiring beyond belief.

"Hey, what do you make of this?" Noah asked, snapping her back to the present. "I think I found your mysterious package."

"The one from the van?" she asked excitedly.

"Take a look."

He carried the monitoring device over to the hatch, turning the screen her way. He pressed a key and a short segment of video began playing.

The deserted downstairs hall at Monique Larousse popped into view. Suddenly one of the side doors opened and a big bald man walked into the hall, a long, plastic-wrapped parcel in his arms.

"That's Arnaud, and that's the package!" Sydney cried, no doubt in her mind.

"Keep watching," Noah advised.

Arnaud headed for the indoor staircase, then hesitated. A moment later, he dropped the package on the floor and began tearing off its black plastic. Sydney strained forward over the steering wheel, catching a thrilling glimpse of crimson before Arnaud unwound the remaining wrapping in one long piece, revealing a long, heavy bolt of red fabric.

"Great," she groaned, disappointed. "Better report straight to headquarters with that exciting intel."

"He comes back later and takes the plastic out the back door. I think he was just trying to save himself a mess upstairs—which is lucky for us, because none of the upstairs cameras are working."

"None of them?"

"Nope. Only the one you're looking at and the one inside the stairwell. And neither one caught a thing."

"Don't you think that's kind of weird?" she asked. "I mean, that all three upstairs cameras are broken when the two that aren't on that floor work?"

Noah nodded slowly. "Yes. I think it's pretty weird. There are ways of knocking out camera signals . . . types of interference devices. SD-6 has a few, but only for small areas and only for minutes at a time. We don't have anything that could take out a whole floor and keep it dark this many hours." He paused, then added ruefully, "At least, nothing that I know of."

"If we had it, I'm sure you'd know."

Noah laughed with disbelief. "You are so innocent. Try to remember that the CIA is in the business of *collecting* information, not giving it out—even to us. Sometimes it feels like the deeper I get, the less I know."

"So what do we do now?" Sydney asked. "Go back with more cameras?"

"Maybe. Here, put these on," he said, holding out the headphones. "We picked up one weird thing, anyway."

Sydney took her hands off the wheel long enough to slip the headphones on over the back of her neck, tilting the pads up to her ears while leaving her hat on.

"This came off the bug in your dressing room," Noah told her, cueing up a sound. "To tell you the truth, I thought it was a waste to drop a bug in there—too public—but this is the only interesting thing we recorded off any of them."

He pressed a key and the playback began.

For a moment, there was only silence. Then Sydney heard faint footsteps. Hinges squeaked; a door closed quietly. The footsteps resumed, more loudly—someone had entered the dressing room. A few more steps, a strange prolonged scraping sound . . . then nothing. Sydney listened a full minute longer, but couldn't hear a thing.

"What do you think that noise was?" she asked Noah.

He shook his head. "And it's silent like that to the end of the playback. It's as if someone has just disappeared."

Sydney started. "That K-Directorate agent," she remembered. "The one they saw go in and never come out . . ."

"Intriguing, isn't it?"

Noah recued the playback so Sydney could hear it again. "You saw that dressing room and I didn't," he said. "Can you think of anything in there that might make that noise?"

"Not really." Her mind was still roaming back over the items in the dressing room, testing each one against the strange sound, when all of a sudden she noticed something that made her forget everything else.

"Noah!" she whispered urgently. "A boat!"

Behind them and to their left, a small boat had crept to within fifty feet of their stern. And unlike every other vessel on the river, this one had no lights on, not even the mandatory safety lights. Its hull was barely more than a shadow against the dark water.

"Hit it!" Noah cried, tossing the monitoring device into the cabin. The attached headphones yanked off Sydney's ears and clattered down the gangway. Lunging up to the deck, Noah grabbed the throttle and pushed it all the way forward.

The engine belched smoke as it roared to full speed. Sydney gripped the wheel, thrown backward by the unexpected change in velocity. Her hat flew overboard, taking the sunglasses perched on its brim along with it. Recovering her balance, she did her best to steer as they rocketed down the Seine.

"Isn't this a little conspicuous?" she shouted to Noah over the engine.

"Not if they're not . . . Yep. Here they come!"

Sydney glanced anxiously over her shoulder. The small boat had turned on its lights and was now pursuing at top speed. The distance Sydney had opened between them was already closing.

"You have to weave," Noah yelled, kneeling at the back of the boat and drawing his gun. "We can't outrun them, so you have to lose them."

"How am I going to lose them on a straight river?" she demanded, panicking.

Noah's elbows were already braced on the back

rail, his gun trained on the approaching boat. "You're the driver. Figure it out."

Sydney held the wheel tightly as the boats raced down the river. Between the noise of their engines and the V-shaped wakes behind them, it seemed impossible that the police wouldn't join the chase any minute.

Which might not be a bad thing, Sydney thought. At least the French police wouldn't kill them; she wasn't sure the same was true of whoever was driving the other boat.

"They're catching up. Do something!" Noah barked.

Sydney cranked the wheel hard to the left, spinning it hand over hand as far as it would go. The back end of the boat slipped wildly over the water, fishtailing out of control. Desperate, she began steering in the opposite direction, but the boat had already made a 270-degree turn and was now speeding straight toward the bank. She corrected her steering barely in time to get the bow pointed back upriver, retracing their earlier path.

"Yes! Good!" Noah shouted encouragement.

Sydney's pulse pounded in her throat, and given five spare seconds, she was certain she'd throw up. Fear and adrenaline mixed like a cocktail in her blood, leaving her barely able to stand.

She glanced behind her. The other boat had made the turn as well, but had lost ground in the process. In front of her, the river forked again. Cranking the wheel, Sydney veered to the right, leaving a small island on her left. The other boat, with more time to react, had no problem following.

"This is Île Saint-Louis," Noah yelled over his shoulder at her. "The island with Notre Dame is right in front of this one. Duck down the passage between them, and maybe we can lose these guys."

No sooner had he spoken than Sydney saw the narrow waterway coming up on her left. The pursuing boat was back up to full speed and had already closed to within yards. Holding her breath, she spun the wheel to the left. The stern started to slide again. . . .

"We're not going to make it!" she cried to Noah.

The short, narrow stretch of river between the two islands lay at an angle that required almost a full U-turn. Sydney's boat was going to clear ninety degrees, at best, then crash into the bank.

"Keep turning!" Noah shouted.

Every bit of her strength went into turning the wheel a little harder, a little farther. The bank of the island rushed toward her, not the soft gradual slope of a natural riverbed, but a concrete wall a few feet high. The bow was still coming around . . . but would it be enough?

Sydney barely avoided a head-on collision with the island, only to have the stern of her boat swing around and hit the wall, knocking her off her feet. She sprawled on the rough-textured deck, scraping her hands and legs, as the boat continued forward on its own.

Noah sprang up and grabbed the wheel. "Are you okay?" he shouted.

Sydney struggled to her knees and looked behind them. The pursuing boat was having the same trouble trying to make the turn, but at its faster speed, it wasn't as lucky. It slammed into the bank sideways, bounced back toward the center of the river, and burst into flames.

Noah killed their engine and turned to look at the flaming wreck. "Nice driving," he said calmly.

Sydney tried to stand, but her legs buckled beneath her. Every part of her body was shaking. From her knees on the deck, she watched the fire on the other boat grow, its flames licking skyward.

That could have been us, she thought.

And then she saw something else. Silhouetted against the blaze, a single dark figure dove into the water and began swimming away.

Noah saw it too and immediately started their

engine, but by the time he'd turned their boat around, the swimmer was lost in the darkness.

He turned to Sydney, his expression grim.

"Well, it's official," he told her. "This isn't a re-con anymore."

10

"CAN YOU TAKE THE wheel again?" Noah asked.

He had steered their boat away from the islands to the center of the Seine, and they had been chugging west for some time now, keeping their speed slow to avoid attracting attention. Sydney could hear sirens behind them, but their wails were gradually receding, and her body had finally stopped trembling, leaving her numb and drained. None of it seemed real anymore—not SD-6, not K-Directorate, and certainly not the insane boat chase she'd just been involved in. Nodding, she reclaimed her position at the wheel.

Noah immediately disappeared down the hatch, reappearing moments later with the laptop monitoring device and headphones.

"Take us right out there, where it's deepest," he told her, pointing. When Sydney reached the spot, he dropped the equipment overboard.

"Aren't we going to need that?" she asked as it hit the water.

Noah shrugged. "Can't carry it with us, and sure can't leave it on the boat."

She nodded, suddenly glad that he was in charge. In her current state, she felt incapable of making the smallest decision; it was all she could do to keep standing.

As they reapproached the dock from which they'd departed, Noah took over the wheel. Sydney jumped off and tied the bowline to a cleat.

"How badly do you think I wrecked it?" she asked, pointing to the stern as Noah joined her on the dock. The side that had crashed into the island was turned toward the water, making it impossible to assess the damage.

"It still floats, and it still runs," he said, unconcerned. "Believe me, that guy's not going to complain. Come on."

He ran off down the dock, leaving Sydney no choice but to follow.

Up on the street, Noah succeeded in hailing a taxi almost immediately.

"Nous allons au Cimetière du Père Lachaise," he fired at the driver as he yanked the door open. *"Dépêchez-vous! Je vous payerai le double si vous y arrivez rapidement."*

Sydney was barely inside before the cab screeched off, rocking them backward against the upholstered seat.

"Noah!" she exclaimed with wonder.

"What?"

"You speak French!"

He grimaced. "I've been speaking it the whole time."

"Yeah, badly. But just now—"

He cut her off with a shake of his head and a worried glance at the driver. "Tell me later."

Sydney stopped asking questions, but her eyes didn't leave his face.

He was faking that lousy accent as part of his cover, she realized. His true accent, the one she'd heard just now, was perfect. The discovery only added to her growing respect for him. Whatever she'd imagined about Noah, he was proving to be even more.

The rest of the taxi ride passed in silence, the driver concentrating on maintaining maximum speed while Noah leaned forward and peered through the windshield, clearly willing the man to go faster still. Sydney slumped wearily in the back-seat, letting the streets slip past without attempting to figure out where they were headed. Noah obviously had a plan, and she'd learn what it was soon enough.

She felt less confident a few minutes later, when the taxi turned down a deserted side street and stopped in the middle of nowhere.

"Nous voici!" the driver announced, turning expectantly to Noah.

In contrast to the bright lights of the city, the land in front of the cab had been swallowed up by darkness. Sydney cleared the condensation from inside her window, but still couldn't see anything.

Noah threw some money at the driver, grabbed her hand, and yanked her out of the car. They were at a cemetery.

"You've got to be kidding," she said as the cab disappeared. "What are we doing here?"

"You'll see," Noah told her, hurrying toward the fence.

"Not to burst your bubble, but I don't think these are visiting hours."

Noah turned just long enough to give her his in-command look. Sydney sighed and climbed up the fence behind him, dropping silently to the other side.

The Cimetière du Père Lachaise was enormous, shrouded in night, and filled with ornate tombs—creepy in the extreme. The scattering of stars overhead did nothing to light their way, and a slice of yellow moon only made the shadows darker. Sydney stuck close to Noah as he darted stealthily from tomb to tomb, keeping a lookout for guards.

They were deep in the cemetery when Noah stopped under the overhanging entrance of an especially large family tomb. He glanced around to make sure they were still unobserved, then turned to face the iron entry door. Massive, black, and flaking with rust, it appeared to have been shut for a hundred years. A heavy knocker hung at its center. Noah lifted the knocker's iron ring, but instead of dropping it, he pushed it up and propped it against the door. Then, kneeling swiftly, he pressed his hand to the door's bottom panel.

To Sydney's amazement, the panel began to glow. She watched as a horizontal beam swept from top to bottom, scanning Noah's palm. A loud click broke the silence, and the door swung open on its own.

"Hurry," Noah urged, grabbing her hand and pulling her into the pitch-black tomb. The door closed heavily behind them with an unmistakable latching sound.

"What is this place?" Sydney whispered, shocked.

"SD-6 safe house," Noah answered in his normal voice. "Totally soundproof, bulletproof, and full of stuff we need." He paused, and when he spoke again, his tone had become more formal. "Computer, voice recognition, Agent Noah Hicks."

A red light switched on overhead, revealing a small rectangular space. Behind them was the wall of the closed entrance door, and directly in front of them another wall was patchworked with memorial stones covering individual coffin cells. Sydney started at the eerie, unexpected sight.

"This is a safe house?" she said uncertainly. She had heard of such places—secret refuges scattered throughout the world—but she hadn't imagined they'd look like this.

Noah reached out and pressed his thumb to an engraving. Another scan, and the entire coffin wall retracted silently into the floor, a false front for the tomb's true contents.

They were now standing in a windowless room about ten feet square. Shelves along the left wall were packed with gear. On the right-hand side, a few stacked boxes leaned against a tarp-covered pile in the corner. Noah strode in, grabbed a black backpack off a hook, and tossed it to Sydney.

"Get what you need," he said, "because we're not going back to the hotel."

Turning his attention to the shelves, he began digging through the equipment, tossing the gear he wanted down to the floor.

"Well? Get busy," he prodded when Sydney didn't move. "Here. I think these pants will fit you." He threw some black stretch pants in her direction, followed by a matching turtleneck. "Better try on some of these shoes, too. The ones you're wearing are useless for running."

Turning her back on Noah, Sydney changed clothes hurriedly, pulling the pants on beneath her dress before shucking that off in favor of the turtleneck. She folded her designer clothes and put them in her backpack with her sandals, in case she needed them later. When she turned around again, Noah was wearing black pants too, but that was as far as he'd gotten. His bare torso flexed as he reached for an upper shelf and pulled down a couple of small plastic cases. She averted her eyes, embarrassed, but he didn't seem to notice.

"Transmitters," he explained, snapping each case open and checking its contents. When he was satisfied, he handed one to her. "Grab one of those utility belts and strap the power box on, then run this wire up to the mike and earpiece."

Sydney did as Noah said while he found a shirt for himself. Unlike the tiny, disguised transmitters they had worn earlier, the new ones were heavy and quite visible. The power box hugged the small of her back, the earpiece clipped over the outside of her ear, and the attached microphone curved around her cheek toward her mouth.

"I feel like a rock star," she joked. "Only without the fans."

Noah smiled appreciatively. "You're in the right place for it. Jim Morrison's buried here somewhere."

Sydney's return smile was weak. Being a rock star was one thing; being a dead rock star didn't seem quite as funny just then. Joining Noah at the shelves, she found a pair of black running shoes and some socks. She was still threading the laces when Noah bent into her line of sight.

"Which gun do you want?" he asked, a weapon held out in each hand.

"Gun?" she repeated. "For what?"

"For our trip back to Madame Monique's, of course. We've got to get in and search the place before K-Directorate has time to cover its tracks."

"We're going in armed?"

Noah looked incredulous. "Well . . . yeah."

Sydney blindly grabbed the nearest weapon. She'd been taught how to shoot them both, but hadn't worked with either one long enough to have an opinion. When she made full agent, she'd be issued a gun, but the only time trainees ever touched one was at the practice range. Until now.

Noah tossed her the holster that went with her choice. "Make sure you have plenty of ammunition. And hurry up—we're wasting time."

Sydney strapped on the gun, praying she wouldn't have to use it. She'd been sent to Paris to shop for clothes, and soon she'd be breaking and entering. The way things were escalating, there was no telling where they'd end.

Looking through the shelves for the right ammunition, she found a locksmith's set, which she added to her backpack. She was already a whiz at picking locks, and they were sure to encounter locked doors at the couture house. Noah helped himself to a pair of night-vision binoculars, and they both took flashlights that hooked to their utility belts. Noah tucked a second gun into his waistband and a third into a leg holster. They finished their outfits with loose black windbreakers that covered most of their equipment.

"Are you ready?" Noah asked, pulling on his backpack over his jacket.

Sydney nodded.

“Good.”

Grabbing the tarp in the corner, he gave it a hard yank. The fabric fell to the floor, revealing a motorcycle and two helmets. He tossed her a helmet and put on the other before wheeling the vehicle into the open space near the center of the safe house. Swinging a leg over the seat, he motioned for Sydney to climb on behind him.

“Hang on tight,” he instructed. “Don’t be shy.”

His voice came to her clearly through their transmitters, but she could no longer see his eyes to tell if he was teasing. Her arms closed tightly around him anyway, crushing his backpack between them.

“I hope you don’t have any guns in there,” she muttered nervously.

“Just hand grenades.”

“What? Noah!”

“I’m kidding,” he said, trying to twist far enough to see her. “Ever hear of gallows humor?”

“The jokes people crack while they’re marching to their executions? That’s perfect. Thanks for the pep talk.”

“No! It’s just . . . never mind. You’re so high-strung.”

“*I’m* high-strung?” she repeated disbelievingly.

He turned back toward the front of the bike. “Are you ready to go, or what?”

"I said I was."

"Fine." Noah started the motorcycle. "Computer!" he called loudly. "Initiate exit procedure."

The red light switched off overhead, the big tomb door swung open, and Sydney and Noah roared out into the night.

* * *

The second time Noah took a corner at top speed, Sydney knew to lean into it with him. She had almost fallen off the bike the first time, and her heart was still thumping from the experience.

I wish I knew when we were going to get there, she thought nervously. Aside from a split-second pause to unlock a cemetery gate, Noah hadn't slowed once since they'd left the safe house. They had to be nearing the couturier's shop by now.

I wish I knew what we'll find.

Would they have to use the guns they carried? Noah obviously took working with weapons for granted, but the thought of actually shooting someone made Sydney feel sick to her stomach. The only thing worse would be if somebody shot her.

This wasn't supposed to be dangerous! she wanted to wail. *Wilson would have an aneurysm if he saw me right now.*

Or would he?

After all, she had signed on to be a secret agent, and Wilson had trained her for the job. Maybe he already knew exactly what was happening.

The lights of Paris streaked past her, as out of focus as her own scattered mind. Sydney took a deep breath.

What I ought to concentrate on is what I'm going to do when we get there.

Except that she didn't know that. She wasn't in charge of that.

The important thing is not to panic. Noah's survived plenty of missions—he's not going to get anyone killed.

Probably.

Another deep breath. The night air was so cool and crisp, it tingled on every nerve. Sydney concentrated on her senses, trying to force the future from her mind. The whine of the motorcycle in her ears, the smell of old stone and exhaust fumes, the warmth of Noah's body against hers, the sharp edges of the lights up ahead . . .

This isn't working.

Every heightened sense only made her more aware that this could be the last night of her life.

"We're about a minute out," Noah's voice said in her ear. "Expect to move fast when we get there."

She nodded stiffly, forgetting that he couldn't see her.

The entrance to the familiar alley came into sight, and Noah took the turn at full throttle. The motorcycle's engine echoed loudly off the building walls as they zoomed up behind the fashion house. Sydney staggered off the bike as it stopped, barely feeling her feet hit the ground. Her legs moved automatically, as if they belonged to someone else. Dropping the motorcycle, Noah led the charge down the exterior stairs to the locked basement door.

They both shed their helmets in the stairway. Sydney reached for her pack to retrieve the locksmith tools, but Noah pulled out a silenced gun and shot the doorknob off.

"It's not really about stealth at this point," he said, kicking the door open. "Come on, Sydney. Let's go!"

They drew their flashlights as Sydney led the race along the downstairs hall, up the staircase, and onto the main floor.

"Which way to the dressing room?" he asked. "Let's move, before someone finds us."

Up ahead, the curtain that had previously separated the back hallway from the rest of the store was now drawn halfway. Sydney blew past it and in a couple more steps entered the main hall, the one the dressing rooms opened onto. She swept her flashlight down its length, to make sure no one was there, then continued straight across it, through an open dressing room door.

"This is the one. This is the room I was in," she told Noah, her voice low and urgent.

"Good. Start looking for things that could have made that noise."

They both began searching, their flashlights playing over the mirrors and furniture. Sydney easily opened each drawer in the tall bureau, but found only sewing supplies. Noah tried rotating the standing mirrors on their hinges, also with no success.

"What could it have been?" he growled impatiently.

Sydney looked around; there weren't many more possibilities. She tried pushing one of the brocade chairs across the hardwood floor. The sound it made was similar to the scraping the bug had recorded, but not nearly loud enough. Taking her cue, Noah shoved the large bureau, only to find it attached to the floor.

"That's going nowhere," he grunted.

"It did sound like something scraping on the wood, though. Could any of these floorboards be loose?"

They dropped to their knees, knocking and prodding. Every board in the floor remained stubbornly fixed. Then Sydney noticed something: At the edge of the floor on one side of the room, a strange, arcing groove was gouged into the wood, ending at the paneled wall.

"What do you think caused this?" she asked.

Noah's eyes lit up. "Bingo."

Leaning into the wall, he ran his palms up and down the vertical boards of the wooden paneling. He had been working only a minute when one of the boards seemed to yield to his pressure.

"Prepare to be dazzled," he said, giving the wall a hard shove. A three-foot-wide section of paneling rotated on an off-center vertical pivot, squealing as twenty-four inches of hidden doorway scraped forward over the hardwood floor.

"A secret passage!" Sydney gasped, rushing forward.

Grabbing her jacket, Noah yanked her back and shone his flashlight into the dark passageway. Two feet behind the paneling was the brick outer wall of the building. A narrow wooden staircase dove steeply to the left, disappearing into darkness.

"I'm going in," he said. "You stay and cover me."

"I'm going with you."

“No,” he said firmly. “You’re not.”

“I want to see what’s down there,” she insisted, more afraid of being left alone than of anything they might face together.

“I understand. But I need you up here, to watch my back. Now turn off your flashlight, get out your gun, and do your job.”

He was gone before she could argue, hurrying out of sight down the rickety staircase. Sydney hesitated, every cell in her body straining to follow. Then she switched off her flashlight and drew her weapon, as Noah had instructed. Her gun shook in her hand.

I can do this, she told herself, fighting to stay calm.

But what if somebody came and she actually had to shoot him? She’d had plenty of weapons training; she knew she could make Swiss cheese of a target.

She just didn’t know whether she could shoot a fellow human being.

“Noah!” she whispered into her transmitter. “Noah, can you hear me?”

“Loud and clear,” he replied.

She relaxed a bit at the sound of his voice. “What’s down there? Are you all right?”

“Yes. I’m just—”

His transmission was cut short by a sudden, sickening thud. Sydney's stomach jerked into her rib cage.

"Noah?" she whimpered, trembling. "Noah, are you okay?"

All she heard was silence.

"NOAH . . . NOAH . . . *NOAH!*"

At the top of the secret staircase, Sydney whispered frantically into her transmitter, immobilized by fear. The way Noah's voice had cut out, it sounded like someone had hit him.

"Noah! Please answer me!"

Her earpiece remained silent. She wasn't even certain their transmitters were still working. Maybe Noah's equipment had malfunctioned. Or been broken.

Or maybe he was dead.

No! No, don't even think that, she told herself,

in a desperate bid to stay calm. Her hands were already shaking; what if she had to shoot?

I need to help him. I need a plan.

But what? If someone had overpowered an experienced agent like Noah, what chance did a trainee have? Was she just supposed to run in shooting and hope for the best?

He'd do it for you, she thought, and somehow she knew she was right. Rescuing Noah might be suicide, but she still had to try.

Summoning up all her courage, Sydney stepped into the passageway. She was reaching for her flashlight when a sudden sound from below made her freeze where she was. Footsteps were rushing up the stairs, directly toward her. Sydney jerked back quickly. Something told her those footsteps weren't Noah's.

She looked frantically for a place to hide, but found no cover in the dressing room. The footsteps were growing louder. Running desperately into the hallway, she noticed the half-drawn dividing curtain ahead. In a few more steps she was behind it, her back pressed to the wall and her chest heaving to her tucked chin.

A beam of light emerged from the passageway and swept back and forth, searching the dressing room. Sydney watched it through the crack where the curtain met the wall. She couldn't see much, just enough to tell that the figure with the flashlight wasn't Noah. And while one of the enemy's hands held a light, the other pointed a gun.

This is bad, Sydney thought, on the verge of panic. Her hiding place wasn't hard to find, and it definitely wasn't bulletproof. One false move, one little noise . . .

She held her breath as the black-clad agent emerged from the dressing room. The flashlight shone down the back hall, past the curtain where she was hiding. A paralyzed Sydney closed her eyes, waiting for the bullet. . . .

Then the light turned and aimed down the main hall instead. Sydney dared to look again, just in time to catch a glimpse of her adversary. The agent was a woman, soaking wet and wearing a bulletproof vest. She swept her light toward the ceiling, illuminating her own pale face and dripping black hair, and Sydney choked back a gasp.

The woman was Monique Larousse!

Agent Larousse, if that was her real name, moved off down the main hallway, leaving Sydney shaking behind her. She listened gratefully as the enemy's squelching footsteps retreated. And suddenly, she had a plan.

Dashing silently across the hall behind

Larousse, Sydney slipped into the secret passageway and raced down the narrow staircase to Noah. The beam of her flashlight bounced crazily off the passage walls as she took the stairs two at a time. There was no time to be careful. She had to get to Noah before Monique Larousse returned.

The staircase ended abruptly. Sydney tripped and fell to one knee on the irregular floor of a square, sloping tunnel. Regularly spaced wooden shoring braced the damp soil walls and ceiling, but the only light was the one in her hand. Recovering her footing, she rushed ahead, intent on finding Noah.

The tunnel stretched on until Sydney lost all sense of how far she had gone. Then suddenly she came to a fork. She hesitated, shining her light down each passageway in turn. Which one should she take?

A low groan from the left-hand tunnel decided her in an instant. Forgetting everything else, she hurtled toward the sound. A dim light appeared up ahead. Then, fifty feet from the fork, the passage ended and Sydney burst into a reinforced steel room. A single bare lightbulb hung from its ceiling, letting her see the whole place at one glance—tall shelving units attached to the walls and neat stacks of crates on the floor.

And there, sprawled on his belly in the middle of it all, was Noah.

"Noah!" she cried, rushing forward and falling to the wet metal floor beside him. Cold water soaked her knees, but Sydney barely noticed as she leaned over her fallen partner, bringing her face close to his.

He groaned again, just barely conscious. Blood trickled down his forehead from a cut on his scalp, and one of his wrists was handcuffed to a steel ring in the floor. She checked for his guns—all three were gone, along with his backpack and jacket. His transmitter lay broken nearby.

"I'm going to get you out of here," she promised, speaking right next to his ear. "Just hang on, Noah. Give me a chance."

Dropping her flashlight, she shrugged off her backpack, removed her locksmith tools, and got to work on his handcuffs. Her hands, which had been shaking ever since she'd entered the fashion house, suddenly became rock steady. She picked the lock in seconds flat, springing the cuff like a pro.

"Come on. Wake up, Noah," she pleaded, dragging him into a sitting position. He slumped against her shoulder, his head lolling on his limp neck.

She shook him gently, then harder, panic rising again.

What if he can't walk?

She might be able to drag him through the tunnel, but not up those stairs.

"Noah, wake up. I'm not kidding!"

His glazed eyes finally opened. He blinked at her, confused.

"It's me. Sydney," she said urgently. "Do you remember?"

He squinted a long time. Then something finally clicked in his gaze. He touched a hand to his injured head and stared at the blood on his fingers. When he looked at her again, he was smiling.

"Way to go, Bristow!" he said admiringly. "Your first real mission and you've already bagged an enemy agent."

"Bagged?" she repeated uneasily, glancing toward the tunnel.

"Yeah. What did you do with Madame Monique? Is she dead? Or did you just knock her out and tie her up?"

"Um . . ."

Noah rubbed his sore wrist, his expression almost jovial. "Personally, I'm hoping for beat her to a pulp and then killed her, but so long as she's not coming back here I—"

"I didn't kill her," Sydney interrupted.

Noah shrugged. "So she's just tied up. It's a loose end, but—"

"I didn't do *anything* to her," Sydney said urgently. "I hid in the hallway until she passed, and then I ran straight down here. We have to hurry."

"You did *what*?" Noah's eyes snapped fully open, no longer the least bit cheerful. "You mean to tell me she's still walking around out there? Armed?"

"I don't know where she is," Sydney admitted. "We have to leave before she comes back."

"And how are we supposed to do that?" he demanded, struggling to his feet. "How are we supposed to get out of here without seeing her again?"

"If we hurry—"

Noah shook his head impatiently. "I have no weapons, you have one, and for all we know, Larousse went to call in her backup. Do you really want to meet up with them in that tunnel?"

Considering the risk she'd just taken for him, it seemed to Sydney that Noah could be more grateful.

"You're right. I probably should have left you down here," she said.

He opened his mouth to speak, then abruptly shut it again. Turning to the first metal shelving unit, he yanked aside a tarp and stood surveying its exposed contents. Sydney saw automatic weapons, heavy artillery shells, and even rocket launchers. Based on her CIA training, she judged the equipment to be Russian, and not of the most recent issue.

"Well, at least we know what they're up to now," Noah said sarcastically. "There's nothing like gunrunning for raising extra cash."

"Where do you think they got this stuff?"

Noah shrugged. "It could be K-Directorate's castoffs. Or maybe they lifted it from the military. Either way, it solves my problem."

Snatching an Uzi off the shelf, he began searching for ammunition. "Check in those boxes," he told Sydney, pointing. "If I can get this loaded, old Madame Monique had better look out."

Sydney hurried to the stacks of metal crates—and found four big cardboard boxes completely full of cash. None of the currencies was familiar, but the quantities were amazing.

"Look at all the money!" she gasped, holding up a bundled stack of bills. "What country is this from?"

"Not one we want armed," Noah said grimly, crossing to her side. "Here, watch out. These must be the ammunition cases."

He tried the nearest metal crate, only to find it locked. The barrel-style combination device under its handle was composed of seven numbered dials, all of which had to be turned to the proper position before the case could be opened. Noah spun them wildly while Sydney started checking other cases.

All of them were locked.

"Give me your extra ammunition," Noah said suddenly, abandoning the cases to run back to the shelves. "Maybe I can find another gun your bullets will work in."

She had barely retrieved her backpack when a noise down the passageway made them both freeze. Footsteps were coming—*lots* of footsteps.

And now they heard voices as well. A woman spoke and a man answered. More male voices jumped into the mix, arguing in Russian. Three men altogether—and not one of them seemed afraid of being overheard.

Sydney drew her gun and pointed it at the open doorway.

"They think it's just you down here, helpless," she whispered to Noah.

Noah nodded, a trapped look on his face. "They've got the helpless part right."

12

"WHAT ARE WE GOING to do?" Sydney asked desperately, her lone gun still trained on the doorway. The voices of the K-Directorate agents were getting louder by the second, and she was sure there were four of them now. "Noah! Do something!"

He cast about the room in a panic, looking for something to use in a fight. The problem was, there wasn't going to be a fight—if all of those agents were armed, there was going to be a slaughter.

Suddenly Noah shouted out. "Sydney! Here we go!"

She turned her head to see him pulling on the

steel ring he'd been cuffed to, swinging up a large section of floor. The ring was the handle to a trapdoor! She ran to him, elated.

And then she looked down.

"It's flooded!" she cried, losing hope.

Inky black water filled the large vertical shaft beneath the trapdoor, rising to within two feet of the metal bunker floor. Any escape that might once have been possible by that route was not an option now.

A flurry of running began in the tunnel; the K-Directorate agents had heard them. Sydney turned anxiously back to Noah—just in time to see him leap into the flooded shaft.

Dark water splashed out and then swallowed him up. The second it took his head to resurface seemed like an eternity. He dog-paddled in the six-foot-square shaft, his head sheltered by the overhanging bunker floor.

"Come on! Get in!" he yelled.

"I'm not jumping in there," she protested, glancing frantically from him to the noisy passageway. "Are you crazy?"

"Get in here *now*!"

His tone left no room to argue—and neither did the approaching agents. Her heart in her throat, Sydney jumped.

Freezing water rushed up past her head. Her feet scrabbled frantically for the bottom, but found only one slimy vertical wall of the chute. The first thing she saw when she surfaced was Noah pulling the trapdoor closed, using a chain on its underside. The heavy steel door clanged into place and Sydney heard a bolt shoot home. The darkness around her was absolute.

"There!" Noah breathed, satisfied. "That ought to hold them a few minutes."

In nearly the same instant, heavy boots clattered onto the floor overhead, accompanied by Russian curses.

"They didn't see *that* coming," Noah added with a chuckle.

"How can you laugh?" Sydney demanded, treading water.

She couldn't see Noah at all—couldn't see her own hand in front of her face—and that he found anything amusing in their situation was impossible to comprehend. Overhead, the K-Directorate agents labored to pull the trapdoor open, temporarily foiled by Noah's locked bolt. The din of their boots echoed painfully in the small airspace between the water's surface and the underside of the bunker floor.

"We're going to die in here!" she said, her voice

rising hysterically. "We're going to drown like rats in a drain!"

"Not if they shoot us first."

As if to underscore his point, a bullet hit the steel over their heads and whined off into the bunker. Agent Larousse barked out something, touching off another argument. Sydney clapped her hands to her ears, her senses overloading with fear.

All of a sudden, a light switched on. Noah had found a row of waterproof flashlights hanging from pegs under the floor. He grabbed a second light and pressed it into Sydney's hand.

"How are you at holding your breath?" he asked.

Sydney's eyes bugged out. She had thought that she couldn't be more terrified, but if she understood what he was proposing . . .

"I am *not* swimming under this water! No way."

The idea of swimming straight down in that vertical shaft took her panic right over the edge. The water was so murky that a flashlight would be almost useless, and there was no way of knowing how long they'd be under—or if they would ever come up. Sydney's breathing went ragged; her body quaked out of control. Noah cupped her cheek with one wet hand, trying to force her to meet his gaze.

"Listen to me," he said. "This is the only way out."

"You don't know that!" she flung back. "You don't know where this chute goes, or if it even goes anywhere!"

Her feet thrashed wildly back and forth, still nothing but water beneath them.

"These flashlights must be here for a reason," he said. "And I like my odds underwater a lot better than up there with those guys."

The trapdoor strained at its bolt again, more significantly this time. One of the agents had found a pry bar to leverage through the ring handle.

Noah stripped off her backpack and jacket, dropping them before she could argue. She felt a tug on her utility belt and it fell away too, yanking her transmitter earpiece down with it.

"What are you doing?" she cried, grasping futilely at her sinking gear. Her gun slipped out of her fumbling fingers and was lost with everything else. Only the waterproof flashlight bobbed back up to the surface.

"You can't swim with all that weight," he said.

"I'm not swimming!" she screamed fearfully.

He pointed his flashlight at her face, staring as if astonished. Then his brown eyes narrowed coldly.

“You’re swimming,” he told her. “This isn’t a negotiation.”

She shook her head determinedly, tears streaming down her face.

He tightened his grip on her cheek. “If you stay here, you’ll die. They’re going to get that trapdoor open and kill you. Now dive.”

“No.”

“No?” His expression became so angry she had to look away.

“I can’t,” she whimpered. “I won’t.”

For a moment the only sounds were pounding boots and the prying overhead. Then Noah let go of her face.

“Suit yourself,” he said, disgusted. “I don’t have time for this rookie crap.”

He dove, both he and his beam of light disappearing at the same time.

Sydney was left behind, alone in total darkness. Her groping hands recovered the floating flashlight, but several seconds passed before she rallied enough to switch it on. Reaching up over her head, she fingered the trapdoor bolt. If she were to open the door and surrender, would they kill her anyway?

A stinging barrage of bullets thundered down on the steel door. She snatched back her smarting hand, any thought of surrendering now abandoned. They *would* kill her—and probably torture her first. Noah had been right; swimming underwater was her only chance. But for her, underwater was no chance at all. Lowering her flashlight beneath the surface, Sydney shone it straight down. Its beam was all but swallowed up, barely illuminating her kicking feet in the darkness that swirled around them. She was choking back sobs as she drew her last breath and forced herself to sink, the light dangling uselessly from her wrist.

The freezing black water closed over her head, extinguishing her last hope. She couldn't see, couldn't think. Above her was a small army of gun-toting K-Directorate; below her, darkness and certain death. She was paralyzed by fear.

Suddenly, a hand reached up and grabbed her, pulling her down, down, down, ignoring her feeble attempts to kick. Her final gasp of air burned in her lungs. In less than a minute, she'd have to breathe. Reflex would force her mouth open, and she'd suck down water instead of air. To die like this, in a foreign country, unknown and unclaimed . . . in the dark . . .

Another hand grabbed her wrist, the one that held the forgotten flashlight, and pointed it to a spot directly in front of her—a horizontal connecting tunnel.

Sydney snapped to her senses. Noah had found a way out! He was shining his own light on his face now, motioning for her to follow him into the tunnel. She did, kicking for all she was worth.

The beam of her flashlight barely pierced the murky water in front of her. Bits of black goop floated past her face, stirred up by Noah's passing. The tunnel walls seemed to be closing in. Was the passage really getting narrower, or was it only claustrophobia? She kept her eyes straight ahead and kicked, fighting to control her churning mind. Either she'd reach the way out now or she'd drown trying—she had gone too far to swim back.

Suddenly the tunnel walls fell away. She and Noah emerged into a huge open area. The water was less cloudy here, and Sydney trained her light upward, following Noah's kicking feet. He was heading for the surface! She could see a row of shimmering lights like blurry halos above him. Her lungs were exploding. Her legs felt like lead. But she was so close now. . . .

Her head burst through the surface as she inhaled, breathing in water as well as air. She choked and coughed, but barely noticed.

Somehow she'd just emerged in the Seine.

"You okay?" Noah asked, slapping her on the back. "You breathing?"

She nodded mutely, still looking around in wonder.

"I'm sorry, but you made me do that."

"Thank you," she gasped past the lump in her throat.

The Paris lights were so achingly beautiful. They twinkled all around her like something from a dream. She found herself crying again, the tears running down her face unheeded. There was no cold, no wet, no mission . . . just an overwhelming happiness that she was alive to see this moment.

She had made it. She had survived.

She was just turning back to Noah when something slapped the water inches from their heads.

A bullet.

"DIVE!" NOAH SAID, PUSHING her back under.

Sydney barely had time to grab a breath before they were off again, frog-kicking two feet beneath the surface of the Seine. Noah dropped his flashlight and she did the same, needing both hands more than the light now. When they came up again, they had traveled a long way toward the center of the river.

"Sydney!" Noah hissed. "Keep your head down and drift with the current. When we get to the other bank, we'll look for someplace safe to climb out."

She gave a single nod, took a deep breath, and

dove, just moments before more bullets smacked into the water around her. They sliced through the shallows, trailing bubbles in their wakes, but in the aftermath of her swim through the tunnel, she regarded them with a strange sense of calm. Maybe she had already faced her worst fear, or maybe her body simply didn't have any adrenaline left. Either way, the woman swimming down the Seine now, surfacing only for short, measured breaths, was not the same girl who had been paralyzed by terror back at the fashion house.

She felt set free, at peace with herself and with whatever happened. And even if her sense of well-being didn't last, some instinct told her that fear would never have quite the same hold on her again. She kept track of Noah, but didn't panic when she occasionally lost him in the dark. For the first time in her life she truly believed that she could take care of herself.

"That looks like a good spot," Noah whispered the next time they came up together.

They had drifted far downstream and crossed all but the last twenty feet of the river. The area Noah pointed to was low and unlit, allowing for an easy climb out and, hopefully, a stealthy getaway.

"Where do you think the shooter is?" Sydney whispered back as they breaststroked quietly to shore. No shots had been fired for several minutes, and she dared to hope they had lost their pursuer instead of simply swimming out of range.

"I doubt there's only one," he replied. "If I were Larousse, I'd put at least two people on tracking us down. Even so, they're going to have to cross a bridge, then double back to get here. I plan to be gone by then."

He pulled himself onto the deserted bank and turned to offer a hand to Sydney, but she was already right behind him.

"I'm freezing," she said, her hair and clothes streaming water down to the pavement. "And we stick out like drenched rats."

"Worse than that, we're going to leave a wet trail. Too bad it isn't raining."

Noah took off at a trot, and Sydney followed gladly, too cold to stand still. Their shoes squished and oozed water as they ran, but Sydney was glad she hadn't kicked hers off in the river, the way they'd taught her at summer camp. In a life-or-death situation, a swimmer could reduce drag that way, but she'd known that if she lived, she would end up running.

Besides, we lost everything else, she thought, tailing Noah down a dark side street. *Both backpacks, our guns, all our tools . . .*

The only things she had left were in the money belt around her waist: cash, her passport, and her SD-6 telephone—assuming it still worked after that dunking.

Noah changed direction again, darting down a different, even darker street. Sydney's breathing came faster, but she stayed behind him easily, grateful for her years of track. They leaped a fence, cut through someone's property, then jumped a wall on the other side. In this part of the city there wasn't much greenery, making good hiding places scarce.

Their wet clothes and hair gradually stopped dripping as they ran, scaling additional walls and doubling back to confuse any would-be pursuers. Sydney was totally lost long before Noah led her down an especially narrow street and stopped in the sheltering alcove of a dark doorway.

He bent over his heaving rib cage, more out of breath than she. "Well," he gasped at last. "That was fun."

Sydney eased her head out of the alcove and peered both ways down the street. "I don't see anyone following us."

"No. We ran a pretty good pattern. They'd need a dog or dumb luck to find us now." He took a deep breath and straightened up. "Never rule out luck. We can't stay here long."

"What do we do next?"

"Good question."

"You mean you don't know?" she blurted out.

"This one isn't in the manual, all right? Just give me a couple of minutes."

She waited silently while Noah thought, each second excruciating. She hadn't much liked his in-charge attitude, but seeing him without a plan was worse. Especially when she didn't have one either.

"Okay," he finally said. "Let's look at what we know, and what we can guess. I'm assuming Larousse was driving the boat that chased us. While we were at the cemetery, she caught another boat downriver and beat us to the fashion house arsenal by swimming in through the underwater tunnel."

Sydney nodded. "That makes sense. She was wet, and so was the floor."

"But once she found me, she knew security was breached, so she called in her reinforcements."

"What do you think they're doing right now?"

"Desperately looking for us," he said grimly. "We know their fashion house is a front to run guns and launder the proceeds. That's not news K-Directorate is going to want spread around."

"No."

"If I were running that op, I'd bring most of the heavy stuff in and out by the river at night.

A couple of guys with scuba gear and the right equipment . . ."

"Right. It would be easier."

"And safer. The land entrance is probably mostly for moving cash."

"What do you think K-Directorate is doing with the money?"

Noah shook his head. "Whatever it is, be certain it's bad. Not to mention that those weapons are going to terrorists. Who else is going to buy them?"

Sydney remembered the unusual currencies she'd seen.

"The stuff still in that bunker . . . ," she said worriedly. "You could arm a small country."

"Yeah." Noah took a deep breath. "So either we confiscate it, or we blow it up. And I can't see how confiscating it's an option."

"You can't be thinking of going back there." Sydney was completely exhausted, and they had both lost all their gear. The thought of returning to Monique Larousse made her want to cry. "There are four of them."

"Yeah. Neutralizing all four is going to be tricky," he said thoughtfully. His brows drew together as he considered his options.

Fumbling under her shirt, Sydney retrieved her

cell phone from her money belt and held it out hopefully.

"Can't we just call the police?"

"What? No! Are you crazy?"

"I'm tired!" she snapped. "And I'm out of ideas." She put the phone away, defeated. "What do *you* want to do?"

To her surprise, his features softened. "I'm whipped too, but we're not done yet. K-Directorate has got to be monitoring the police frequencies, and unless Larousse is a fool, she has one or two of those agents on standby right now, just waiting for the word to start moving ops elsewhere. All that stuff could be gone in a couple of hours."

"Even with people still out here looking for us?"

"The fact is, we don't know where anyone is at this point. Which means that we definitely have to get moving. I'd just like to have a plan before we—"

A sudden noise froze Noah in midsentence. Footsteps echoed down the narrow street, striding quickly in their direction. Peering out of the alcove, Sydney spotted the menacing form of a man dressed in black. In a few more seconds, he would be on them.

"Noah, someone's coming!" she whispered frantically. "I think he's—"

Noah slammed her spine into the back of the alcove, covered her body with his, and kissed her passionately.

For a moment her mind went blank. Noah was all over her! His hands braced on either side of her head, he leaned into her hard, pinning her to the wall as his mouth pressed insistently against hers. She stiffened, stunned. Then she realized what it meant.

They were both about to die.

She flung her arms around his neck and willingly kissed him back. They couldn't run; they couldn't hide. If these were their last few moments on earth, at least they wouldn't die alone.

Her fingers traveled up into his hair, closing around two damp handfuls. Her mouth opened to his as he took the kiss deeper. The footsteps slowed just feet away, but Sydney barely heard them. All the tension and passion that had crackled between her and Noah since the moment she'd first seen him had suddenly found its way to their lips. She had never been kissed by anyone the way Noah was kissing her now, and she'd certainly never responded in kind. She tightened her grip on his hair, pulling his mouth down harder on hers. He shifted a hand behind her neck, cupping the base of her head to tilt her lips up farther.

The footsteps stopped. Sydney knew if she opened her eyes, she would see her killer face to face. He probably had a gun aimed at their heads that very second. . . .

She didn't open her eyes. Her hands ran the length of Noah's back and slipped under his shirt, exploring his warm chest. She could feel his heart hammer beneath his skin, pounding in rhythm with hers. They were both breathing like marathon runners.

This is it, she thought.

Suddenly the footsteps resumed and walked away until even the echoes were gone.

Noah released her abruptly, staggering backward. For a moment they both stared, stunned by what had just happened. It had taken a near-death experience to make them tell the truth, but there could be no denying the feelings they'd just revealed. Sydney's empty hands twitched at her sides, itching to pull him back into her arms. Her lips, swollen with his kisses, parted slightly, anticipating his return. . . .

Then Noah started apologizing.

"Wow. Sorry about that," he said, rubbing a hand across his eyes. "I just . . . it had to look real. Was that guy K-Directorate?"

"What?" Her jaw snapped shut.

"You're the one who saw him. I thought you said he was an agent."

"I thought he might be, but—"

"So there was no other way to hide. I never would have otherwise. . . ." Noah shook his head as if to rid himself of the memory. "I mean, you know that, right? All in the line of duty."

"Right. Me too."

Humiliation burned across her cheeks. To think that he hadn't meant any of it, and she had kissed him like *that*. . . .

"Sometimes you have to get physical," he said. "It's the best way to hide in plain sight."

Was he saying he'd done this before? With someone else?

"Of course," she croaked. "Obviously."

"You understand, then," he said, relieved.

"What did you think *I* was doing?" she rallied.

Her answer seemed to set him back. They stared at each other again.

"Good," Noah said at last.

"Good," she repeated, determined not to look pathetic.

"I think we'd better move."

"I agree."

Creeping cautiously out of the alcove, they began running down the street in the opposite direction from the black-clad man. Maybe he had been K-Directorate. Maybe not. But despite what Noah had just said, Sydney remembered the protective way he'd covered her body with his, as if to shield her from a bullet. She remembered the urgency of his kisses, and the answering hunger of hers. . . .

Increasing her pace, she tried to forget. She and Noah had been through a lot together that night. If people got a little caught up in the moment, it didn't necessarily mean anything.

It didn't necessarily mean nothing.

If we live, I'll think about it later, she decided, following Noah into a tiny park.

A cluster of trees near the center provided a decent hiding place, their low-hanging branches a tangle of confused shadows on the grass. Sydney and Noah slipped in among them, their black clothes blending to invisibility.

"There's no time to take a cab back to the cemetery and get new gear," Noah announced as soon as they were hidden. His tone was completely back on the mission. "We have to get guns, but where?"

"Around here?" Sydney gestured to the nothingness surrounding them. "Let's hear your backup plan."

"We have to have weapons," he insisted. "How much money do you have?"

"Lots."

"Things can always be had, for a price. The right bar . . . a bad part of town . . ." His face tensed with concentration. "The problem is, we're losing time. They could be moving that stuff right now."

Sydney tried to think, putting everything else aside. Their lives were at risk, and so was their mission. If they didn't come up with something soon . . .

Suddenly her face lit up.

"I know where we can get guns!" she cried. "And I have another idea too."

Retrieving her phone for the second time, she snapped it open, ready to dial. Noah grabbed her hand, stopping her.

"Hold it," he said sharply. "Anything we decide, we're deciding together."

"READY?" NOAH WHISPERED. "WE'LL only get one chance."

Flat on their bellies on the rooftop of Monique Larousse, Sydney and Noah looked down three stories at the alley behind the fashion house—and at the two K-Directorate agents patrolling it. It hadn't been hard climbing the building at the end of the row and creeping over the rooftops to get to that point. What was going to be hard was getting down.

Sydney took a deep breath. "Ready."

"Let me take Anatolii," Noah said, pointing to

the larger agent. "Are you sure you can handle the other guy?"

I'd better be sure, she thought. *It was my idea.*

Still, taking on an armed K-Directorate agent with only her rookie Krav Maga fighting skills had seemed like a better idea in the park. If he looked up and saw her before she got close enough . . .

Noah sensed her uncertainty. "I'd take them both, but—"

"No, I can do it," she said quickly. "It has to be both of us."

"How's your line?"

Sydney checked the knotted clothesline wrapped around her waist. They had commandeered lengths of the cord from several backyards, along with a blanket for padding, leaving money under doormats for the unsuspecting French homeowners.

"It seems all right," she answered. "You're sure this will slow us down?"

"If nothing I tied it to breaks."

"Noah—"

"It'll work."

They peered over the edge of the building again. The enemy agents were walking a military-style pattern, pacing the alley in opposite directions before returning to cross paths behind the fashion house. The beams of their flashlights swept side to side, ready to pick up anything that moved, while their free hands hovered at the edges of their open jackets, poised to draw their weapons. Noah picked up a handful of gravel as the sentries neared their meeting point.

"Okay," he whispered. "Here we go."

With a sharp, sidearm motion, he hurled the rocks across the alley into the bushy area behind the Dumpster. In the late-night quiet, the gravel ripped through the leaves like a shotgun blast. Both K-Directorate agents whipped their flashlights toward the sound, drawing their guns in unison.

"Now!"

Leaping from the rooftop, their improvised safety ropes unfurling as they fell, Sydney and Noah landed on the enemy agents' backs, knocking them to the ground. The fight Sydney had anticipated was over before it began as her stunned man collapsed to the pavement, his gun and flashlight clattering out of reach. He gasped for air as she relieved him of his handcuffs, using them to secure his hands behind his back. Then she yanked the release knot at her waist, freeing herself of the safety line.

"Clear!" she called, turning to Noah.

Noah was also clear of his line. He had Alek

Anatolii facedown on the pavement and was attempting to handcuff him, but the big man was putting up a fight, struggling wildly beneath the knee Noah had planted in his back. As Sydney watched, Alek flipped Noah off and dove sideways across the pavement, his hands grasping for something just out of reach.

Gun!

The alarm went off in Sydney's brain. Instinct sent her hurtling toward Anatolii. In two steps, she closed the distance between them. On the third, her right foot swung up beneath Alek's chin, connecting with a force that snapped his head backward. He crumpled to the pavement, inert.

Sydney held her breath as Noah rushed over to check Anatolii's pulse. "Did I . . . Is he . . . dead?" she whispered.

"No, but you cleaned his clock pretty good," Noah told her admiringly, slapping a pair of cuffs on the muscular agent. "Come on. Help me take out this trash."

The two of them dragged Anatolii and his partner into the dark space behind the Dumpster, using a third pair of handcuffs to secure both agents to the heavy trash receptacle. Sydney held the flashlight she'd recovered from her man while Noah patted the agents down for weapons. The one Sydney had jumped on groaned semiconsciously; Anatolii never woke up.

"Plenty of illegal hardware on these two," Noah said, grinning at Sydney as he pulled a cigarette lighter out of Anatolii's pocket. "And this ought to make things a whole lot easier for us. Go get the big guns."

Hurrying back to the scene of the fight, Sydney found the weapon Alek had been reaching for and recovered his flashlight too. The other agent's gun was lying nearby. She picked it up just as Noah reappeared at her side.

"Nice of these guys to take care of our gun problem for us," he said, helping himself to a weapon and a flashlight.

Sydney nodded, but secretly she still hoped there wouldn't be shooting—and there wouldn't, if the second part of their plan worked.

"Come on," said Noah. "Let's do this thing."

They ran down the back stairs to the basement door, which was still hanging open from their previous forced entry. Guns in one hand, flashlights in the other, they charged into the downstairs hallway just as the first siren wailed in the distance. They grinned at each other and kept going, racing up the stairs, through the main-floor hallways, and into the dressing room. The secret passageway panel was open. They pushed through sideways and thundered down the hidden stairs on their way to the arsenal.

At the fork in the passageway, Sydney hesitated. "I'm going to check this out," she told Noah. "We ought to know where the other branch goes."

"Okay, but do it fast," he said, running down the left-hand tunnel.

Sydney watched him go, then veered off to the right. The passage narrowed quickly, and seconds later she was shining her light into the dirt wall of a dead end. The tunnel had never been completed, or perhaps it had been a wrong direction in the first place. Turning abruptly, she sprinted back to the fork and hurried to find Noah.

Inside the bunker, a fire blazed on the metal floor. Sydney skidded to a halt at the eerie sight. Firelight flickered up the steel walls, illuminating the weapons stores and casting shadows on the low ceiling. The trapdoor she and Noah had escaped through now stood twisted and open, ripped halfway off its hinges. Noah was standing beside it, throwing K-Directorate's cash on the fire.

"The other tunnel's a dead end," she reported breathlessly.

Noah grinned and tossed her an underwater flashlight. "Good." He picked up a box of shells. "Are you ready?"

Sydney nodded. "Are you?"

Noah dropped the shells into the flames. The fire blazed up around them as he switched on a second flashlight and dove headfirst through the trapdoor, disappearing beneath the dark water. Without hesitation, Sydney dropped her K-Directorate gun and dove in right behind him.

The water in the vertical shaft was just as cold and inky as before, but Sydney barely noticed. Kicking strong and confidently, her flashlight trained in front of her, she reached the horizontal connecting tunnel in seconds, just in time to see Noah's feet disappear inside it.

In the horizontal passage, the visibility was still horrendous, the tunnel walls still far too close. The pain of her need to breathe felt like a knife through her lungs. But Sydney didn't panic. Instead, she kicked with all her strength, determined to make it through a second time. The beam of her flashlight flickered out, sending her heart up into her throat, but it snapped back on a moment later, just as the tunnel ended.

Sydney emerged into the Seine and angled sharply for the surface, knowing she was going to live. She could see Noah above her, kicking steadily. They broke into the cold night air as the first explosion rocked the sleeping city.

A boom like a cannon blast sent shock waves through the river. Treading water beside Noah, Sydney ducked her head, expecting the ensuing din of smaller explosions to fling shrapnel their way.

"Most of the fallout should stay underground," said Noah, reading her mind. "Otherwise we couldn't have risked doing this in the city."

Another huge explosion split the night, its reverberations echoing off buildings on both sides of the Seine. Sirens wailed at full volume, accompanied by shouts and honking horns as emergency vehicles raced to the scene.

"What was that?" cried Sydney. "A bomb?"

Noah grinned. "Isn't that what you told the fire department?"

"And I told you they'd get here fast."

"I'm sure it helped when you said you were going to explode it." He shook his head slightly, his eyes crinkling at the corners. "You're actually starting to amaze me, Bristow. Come on. Let's get out of here and find a better view."

They swam to the nearby bank, letting the current move them downstream, but staying on the same side of the river as the fashion house. The ongoing explosions and sirens were waking the whole city, filling the streets with shouting, frightened people.

It's working, Sydney thought anxiously as she

and Noah pulled themselves out of the water and began running through the dark streets. *So far everything's working. . . .*

Part one of the plan she'd made with Noah was to destroy the arsenal; part two was to neutralize the four agents. To accomplish part two, they needed help—and that was when Sydney had hatched the idea of calling the fire department instead of the police. Using her untraceable cell phone, she had shouted the two French sentences supplied by Noah: "There's a bomb at Monique Larousse. Long live the People's Revolution of God!"

The idea had been to sound like a terrorist, and judging from the panic she'd heard on the line, she'd succeeded. The dispatcher had probably still been scrambling when Noah called back to make his own report in perfect French.

He had just passed a store called Monique Larousse, he claimed, where he had seen a woman climb out a window and run away carrying a can of gasoline. Could he describe her? *Mais oui!* A tall woman dressed all in black, mid-thirties, jet-black hair, milk white skin, and bloodred lipstick.

If they see Agent Larousse tonight, they'll have to pick her up, Sydney thought now, running around a corner. *No one could mistake that description!*

A loud, rapid series of blasts indicated that the

fire had spread into something new. More spectators came running from nearby clubs and hotels. Rotating lights on police and fire vehicles strobed colorfully in the street in front of the fashion house and in the alley behind it. Officers strung crime tape between their cars to form temporary barricades, shouting orders in French and working hard to keep the curious back. Sydney and Noah continued running, turning into the first street beyond the alley.

Here, the explosions were nearly as loud, but there were far fewer people around. Noah found a break between two buildings and leaped, pulling himself up onto a fire escape. Sydney made the jump right behind him, sailing along on one last burst of adrenaline. A moment later, they had climbed to the roof and were peering down into the alley behind Monique Larousse.

"What chaos!" Noah whispered happily. "Let's see if we can get closer." He began creeping along the flat rooftops, staying low and sticking to the shadows.

Sydney followed cautiously, one eye on Noah and one on the action below her. Police and firemen raced back and forth, trying to pinpoint the source of the explosions. No one was being allowed to enter Monique Larousse, but the lower back windows had been broken, whether by explosions or emergency crews, Sydney couldn't tell. Glass glittered on the pavement, pulverized by the boots running over it.

When Noah was almost directly opposite the fashion house, he flattened himself on his belly, motioning for Sydney to do the same.

"Can you see those two K-Directorate agents?" she asked, looking over the edge of the building at the brushy slope. Even with all the flashing lights, the area behind the Dumpster was too dark for her to make out.

Suddenly, a huge explosion shook the ground, sending everyone down below scurrying for cover. A third-story window gave way at Monique Larousse, showering glass into the alley. Bystanders screamed and sirens wailed.

"How long can this keep up?" Sydney asked Noah worriedly.

He shrugged. "So long as it stays underground, who cares?"

He didn't bother to whisper, and she probably couldn't have heard him if he had. Smaller explosions were popping like firecrackers, their echoes pinging off the walls.

The officers had just begun walking upright again when a different kind of commotion began in the alley. Shouting in the distance grew in both volume and urgency as five people came running full speed up the pavement. Monique Larousse and the remaining K-Directorate agent were out in front, and hot on their trail were three policemen yelling in frantic French.

"Madame! Monsieur!"

"Vous ne pouvez pas entrer là!"

"Arrêtez-vous! Revenez!"

Noah turned to Sydney, a disbelieving smile on his lips. "Call me crazy, but I think this is going to work."

Reacting to the shouts of their fellow officers, armed policemen closer to the fashion house formed a line and intercepted the agents before they reached the basement stairs.

"I am Monique Larousse!" Agent Larousse cried, trying to push her way through the officers. "I must get into my building before I lose everything!"

"Too late," Noah said cheerfully.

A rapid conversation in French began, with everyone shouting at the same time. Larousse became increasingly agitated, pointing to her building and indicating the partner at her side. A commanding officer stood back from the commotion, speaking into a walkie-talkie. As Sydney watched, he switched off the instrument, strode forward, and began questioning Agent Larousse.

"What's happening?" Sydney asked Noah desperately.

"He just accused her and her buddy there of arson for insurance fraud," Noah reported, loving it.

Larousse began a frantic rebuttal, waving her arms for emphasis, but before she had finished, the senior officer gave a signal and both she and her partner were handcuffed and forced into a squad car.

In almost the same instant, another shout went up. A junior officer had found Anatolii and the fourth enemy agent handcuffed behind the Dumpster. There was a flurry of activity as floodlights were brought and the situation examined. Noah chuckled as the men were patted down and their concealed guns and other illegal equipment started to emerge. The officers became agitated, drawing their own weapons for cover, and finally the last two K-Directorate agents joined the others in the back of a locked squad car.

It was over.

"We did it!" Sydney hooted triumphantly. "We rock!"

Elated, she held up a hand for Noah to high-five.

But when he turned to look at her, the amazed expression on his face made her hand waver in the air. For the first time in hours, she remembered the difference in their ages—and in their experience.

Oh, no, she thought, heart sinking. *He thinks I'm really young and geeky.*

She felt like a total fool. But before she could lower her hand, Noah slapped it with his own.

"Way to go, Agent Bristow," he said warmly.

He smiled at her and Sydney smiled back, both thrilled and exhilarated.

Agent Bristow, she thought happily. *I like the way that sounds!*

15

THE KNOCK AT SYDNEY'S hotel room door jerked her upright on the bed. She'd been lying on top of the sheets, fully clothed. Now her eyes sought out the bedside clock, provoking a loud groan. She had finally managed to doze off and she'd only been asleep for two hours.

At least I'm already dressed, she thought groggily, swinging her stocking feet down to the carpet and shuffling toward the door. She had wanted to buy clothes the night before, but the stores had been closed at that late hour. She and Noah had been stuck in the black pants and turtlenecks they'd worn on their mission, looking like a couple of mimes without their makeup.

Without any makeup at all, Sydney thought wistfully, smoothing a stray strand of hair behind her ear. Thankfully she'd had the opportunity to shampoo.

She and Noah had checked into the low-budget hotel ridiculously early that Tuesday morning, after sneaking down from their rooftop perch and catching the first available cab headed south. As much as Sydney would have liked to go back to the Plaza Athénée to soak in marble luxury and reclaim her SD-6 wardrobe of designer clothes, Noah hadn't thought it was safe.

"K-Directorate is a lot bigger than four people," he'd reminded her. "That suite could be under surveillance from anywhere in the world."

So instead, they'd used some cash to take separate rooms at the new place. Sydney's room was small but clean, and she'd been so exhausted, she should have been able to sleep standing up. But as it had turned out, she'd also been too keyed up and too wet to relax, instead passing half the night drying her clothes with the hotel hair dryer.

She pulled her door open now to find Noah grinning on the other side, looking as rested as if he'd just come off a two-week vacation. He held a bottle of orange juice in one hand and a newspaper in the other.

"For you," he said, offering her the juice. "How did you sleep?"

Sydney took a long drink before answering his question. "Did I sleep?" she countered, waving him inside and closing the door behind him.

He laughed as he crossed the room and dropped the newspaper on her bed. "Too much fun, huh?"

"Too much fun, and not enough pajamas. How did you sleep in those wet clothes?"

He winked at her. "I didn't."

The obvious implication made her blush. Not that there was anything wrong with sleeping in the nude—she was just pretty sure she shouldn't be thinking about Noah doing it. Or about the way he had kissed her the night before. Or especially about the way she had kissed him back . . .

"I was up for hours using the hair dryer on mine," she volunteered, eager to change the subject. "I finally got them dry, but my shoes are still damp."

Noah made a face. "Seems like a lot of trouble. I just hung mine up and they're okay now. Except for the shoes."

"Yeah. The shoes," she echoed, still too embarrassed to meet his eyes. She finished her juice instead and ditched the bottle on top of the tiny dresser.

"I brought you something to read on the plane," Noah said, picking up the paper and handing it to her. "Check this out."

Sydney scanned the lead headline of the English-language newspaper: FOUR ARRESTED IN SUSPECTED ARMS DEALINGS.

The subsequent article, accompanied by a photograph of the fashion house surrounded by emergency vehicles, anchored the front page.

"If they know about the guns, they must have been able to get down the tunnel," Sydney said, sitting on the edge of the bed to read. "I thought it must have collapsed."

Noah leaned against the wall. "That bunker has to be flattened, and probably flooded too. But the way ammo sounds blowing up . . . the police know what it was. Besides, they have all the time in the world now to dig for evidence. Between what they'll find underground and a look at the books, it's a pretty safe bet that Monique Larousse will never reopen."

"So . . . everyone who worked there . . . Henri, Arnaud, Yvette. They were all K-Directorate?"

"I don't think so. I checked in with SD-6 this morning, and so far only the four we tangled with have turned out to be known agents. Larousse was running the show while Anatolii's squad smuggled the guns and kept order. All those other employees are just clueless French citizens."

Sydney shook her head in disgust.

"Check out the next page. It gets better."

On the second page of the newspaper, a photograph showed all four agents being marched into police headquarters in handcuffs. Agent Larousse's face was shown, although Anatolii had managed to duck. The other two agents were caught in profile.

"That's going to screw up their covers!" Noah gloated. "I'm predicting major plastic surgery before those four work again."

"Work again?" she echoed, shocked.

"K-Directorate will get them out. Did you think they were locked up for good?"

"Well . . . actually . . ."

Noah smiled. "You're so cute when you're naïve. We'll see those four again—and next time they'll be looking to get even. Try not to freak out when I say this, but we probably should have shot them when we had the chance."

Sydney stared at the floor. They both knew she'd been the one who had pushed to get the agents arrested instead.

"I didn't want to kill anyone," she admitted. "It's one thing to shoot in self-defense, but to pick someone off in cold blood . . ."

To her surprise, Noah crossed to the bed and gave her shoulder an awkward pat.

"No one ever *wants* to. . . . Anyway, they're tied up long enough for us both to get out of here. I've got a taxi waiting outside, if you're ready."

"Right now?" she said, taken aback. "It's waiting outside right now?"

"It's amazing what a phone call will do."

"No, but . . . We're going back to L.A. already?"

"You are. SD-6 called the airline and reserved your new ticket. I have a few loose ends to tie up here, but I'll ride with you to the airport."

"Oh," she said, disappointed. "I thought we'd be flying back together."

She had hoped so, anyway. In side-by-side seats on the long ride home from France, she might have been able to muster the courage to ask when she'd see him again . . . and what it would mean when she did.

Noah simply smiled and looked around the hotel room. "So, all packed?"

"Very funny," Sydney replied, pulling on her damp shoes.

* * *

"The good thing about traveling in this direction is you only lose three hours," Noah said as their taxi pulled up at the airport. "You'll still be there in time for your afternoon classes."

He grinned and Sydney knew he was teasing, trying to make her complain about how completely exhausted she was. It would have been easy to do in her current state, but with Noah acting so chipper, she didn't want to look weak.

"Perfect," she said, stepping out to the curb. "I'd rather go today than make up more work later."

Maybe if I sleep on the plane . . ., she thought. *Or even if I sleep during class. At least I can say that I went.*

Anything was better than having Noah think she couldn't cut it as an agent.

Inside the terminal, he guided her to an open shop. Most of the airport stores were closed so early in the morning, but a coffee stand was open, and so was the adjacent souvenir-and-magazine merchant.

"You might want to buy a purse, or some sort of bag," he suggested. "It looks better than taking your passport out of your back pocket."

"Good idea." She'd already made up a story about falling into a hotel swimming pool, in case anyone asked how her passport got wet.

Noah waited outside while Sydney browsed the limited choices in the small gift shop. A couple of plain fanny packs were the closest substitute for a purse. She picked a blue one, knowing anything was better than hiking up her shirt in public to access her hidden money belt. As she walked toward the cash register, she filled the bag with a few essentials: lip gloss, breath mints, a folding hairbrush. A powder blue scrunchie caught her eye and went in too. And there, sitting beside the register, was the best thing in the whole store—an embroidered tote bag depicting the Eiffel Tower and filled to overflowing with fine French chocolate and jams.

"I'll take that, too," she said, pointing impulsively as the sales clerk rang up her purchases.

"Oui, mademoiselle!" he replied, clearly seeing eurodollar signs.

Sydney didn't care. *After what I've been through on this mission, Wilson owes me some jam,* she thought, paying with SD-6 funds.

Emerging from the store, she thrust the tote bag into Noah's hands. "Hold this a second," she said.

"For me?" he asked, mock flattered.

"You wish. I just want to put in this scrunchie." Sydney clipped the fanny pack around her waist with the pouch in front. Stretching the blue fabric loop over her wrist, she began brushing out her hair.

"So you're hungry then," he persisted. "Did they give you a spoon to eat this jam, or do we need to find you one?"

"What are you talking about?"

"Big, touristy tote bag . . . lots of labels in French. Are you planning to tell your roommate you picked this up in San Diego?"

Sydney's face fell. She finished her ponytail and let it drop, then took the tote back from Noah.

"I wasn't thinking," she admitted, bracing for the rookie jokes. "I just wanted a souvenir."

"Well . . . carry it through security, then ask for a big loaf of bread on the plane. It does make you look more normal than walking around empty-handed."

"Right," she said gratefully.

Noah stood in line with her to collect her airplane ticket. She asked for a window seat this time, but there wasn't even a seat left on the aisle.

"Full plane," the ticket agent said apologetically. "I had to put you in a center seat in the center section."

Sydney accepted the ticket without further comment. "Center section?" she asked Noah as they walked away.

"You're not in first class anymore," he told her, shaking his head sadly. "Especially not dressed like that."

"You don't look any better!" she protested.

"No, but I will by this afternoon. Anyway, what do you care? You're going home alive, and that's the main thing."

"I know."

Noah looked ahead to where the passengers were lining up at the security checkpoint. "This is as far as I go."

Stepping out of the path of traffic, he stopped beside a wall.

Sydney stopped beside him. "You're not going to the gate?" she asked, trying not to whine.

"Not without a ticket." He shrugged. "Besides, you'll be sitting there awhile. And I have things to do."

"Oh, right. Of course."

"Okay, then," he said, shrugging again.

"Good-bye. I guess."

Neither of them moved. Sydney's toes curled up inside her shoes with her desperate need to say more.

"It was good working with you," he added. "You'll make a great agent, Bristow. I can tell."

Under different circumstances, a compliment like that would have kept her walking on air for days. Now all she felt was disappointment.

What about us? she wanted to scream. *What about you and me?*

But she just couldn't spit it out. After all, Noah was older than she was, and higher in SD-6. If she was wrong, if she had misinterpreted his feelings, if kissing her really *had* been just a simple cover maneuver . . .

I would die from the humiliation, she concluded. *It's better to let it drop.*

So why was she still standing there?

Noah Hicks could make my life far too complicated. For one thing, there's probably a rule against dating fellow agents. Besides, Dad would have a fit if he found out I was seeing an older man. Or wait . . . maybe that's a plus. Anyway, anyone can see that Noah comes with too much baggage. He's bossy, and proud, and impatient, and . . .

And I might already be half in love with him.

Could she really tell him that? Now? More people were arriving every second, adding to the passing crowd. Sydney's eyes searched his for any clue, any little sign. For a second she thought she saw a flicker. . . .

Then Noah shrugged again.

"So, I'll see you around, I guess," he said. "I mean, I'm sure I'll run into you sometime."

It wasn't much, but for a guy with so many things to do, he sure didn't seem to be in any hurry to leave. She took a step toward him, then stopped, reconsidering.

What if I'm wrong?

"I'll see you," she agreed, settling for a hopeful smile.

She watched him walk away, and when he

turned back to wave good-bye, her breath caught in her chest. There *was* something between them; she just didn't know what it was yet.

I think I'll make it my next mission to find out.

* * *

A finger poked Sydney in the back of the shoulder, startling her out of her daydreams.

"They're not bothering you, are they?" the woman seated directly behind her leaned forward to ask.

"What? Who?"

"My kids," the woman replied, looking at her strangely. She had the center seat between four of her young children, and two more sat to one side of Sydney, wrestling over their shared armrest and putting their tray tables up and down. Dad had the aisle to Sydney's left, a fidgety toddler between them.

"No. They're fine," Sydney assured her, settling back into her seat.

In fact, they were wiggly, wild, and hyped up on the fancy French chocolate Sydney had passed around, but they still weren't bothering her. Wedged into the single leftover seat amidst this big, lively family, she felt the safest she had since she'd left L.A. It was unexpectedly relaxing, being with normal people again.

No one seeing me now would ever guess I live a secret life, she thought, amused. Everything about her current appearance screamed exhausted college student.

International spy? I don't think so.

Anyone who glanced her way might easily mistake her for the family's nanny. No one on the plane would ever know how much she'd just risked to protect them.

And I like it that way, she realized. She didn't want to be thanked, or even recognized; she just wanted to make a difference.

Tugging at her small square pillow, she tried to make herself more comfortable. The plane had only been in the air for an hour, and she could barely keep her eyes open. If she could just find a comfortable place for her head . . .

Am I really going to classes this afternoon? she wondered. She couldn't remember the last time she'd been so tired. Between the jet lag, the lack of sleep, and enough running around Paris to make missing track practice irrelevant, she didn't have anything left. *Even if I don't go, I'll tell Noah I did.*

Except that then I'll be lying again.

There were so many people her new career forced her to lie to already: Francie, her father, everyone at school. Noah was one of the very few with whom she could have a totally honest relationship.

And I want that, she realized. *I want that a lot.*

A person couldn't go through life with no one to confide in. Since they'd met last summer, she and Francie had become fast friends—best friends, really. But now there was always going to be SD-6 between them.

I can't wait to see her, though, Sydney thought drowsily. *And Wilson. Wait till he hears what I've been up to. Wait till I get another crack at that immersion tank!*

She pulled the thin blanket up under her chin, shifting her weight to one hip.

And Noah, she thought dreamily. *I'll definitely be seeing Agent Hicks again. . . .*

Sydney sighed and fell asleep, a satisfied smile on her lips.

ANOTHER MISSION ACCOMPLISHED. I'VE BEEN AGENT HICKS FOR A LONG, LONG TIME. **NOTHING** SURPRISES ME. NOTHING CATCHES ME OFF GUARD. STRESS, RISK, DANGER—IT'S ALL PART OF THE **JOB**.

FALLING IN **LOVE** ISN'T.

NOW AVAILABLE
AS AN AUDIOBOOK ON CD
FROM IMAGINATION STUDIO...
ALIAS
INCLUDES EXCLUSIVE TRADING CARDS FROM INKWORKS!
abc
BASED ON THE HIT ABC SHOW!
©2002 Touchstone Television. All Rights Reserved.
ALIAS
RECRUITED
AN ORIGINAL PREQUEL NOVEL BASED ON THE HIT TV SERIES CREATED BY J. J. ABRAMS
ALIAS
A SECRET LIFE
AN ORIGINAL PREQUEL NOVEL BASED ON THE HIT TV SERIES CREATED BY J. J. ABRAMS
Alias Prequel #1: RECRUITED • Read by Amanda Foreman • 0-8072-1040-4
Alias Prequel #2: A SECRET LIFE • 0-8072-1041-2
Alias Prequel #3: DISAPPEARED • 0-8072-1042-0
abridged • approx 2 hours • 2CD's • $19.99/$29.99 Can
imagination STUDIO
HAVE A LISTEN!
WWW.RANDOMHOUSE.COM/AUDIO